# My Neighbours

# My Neighbours

Caradoc Evans

Edited with an afterword
by
John Harris

Planet

Published
in Wales in 2005

PO Box 44
Aberystwyth
Ceredigion SY23 3ZZ
Cymru/Wales

Design: Glyn Rees

Cover image: Caradoc Evans, Maidenhead, 1933. Photo:
© 2004, TopFoto

Printed by Gwasg Gomer
Llandysul, Ceredigion

ISBN: 0-9540881-5-8

# Contents

# THE TWO APOSTLES

## THE TWO APOSTLES

GOD covered sun, moon, and stars, stilled the growing things of the earth and dried up the waters on the face of the earth, and stopped the roll of the world; and He fixed upon a measure of time in which to judge the peoples, this being the measure which was spoken of as the Day of Judgment.

In the meanseason He summoned Satan to the Judgment Hall, which is at the side of the river that breaks into four heads, and above which, its pulpits stretching beyond the sky, is the Palace of White Shirts, and below which, in deep darknesses, are the frightful regions of the Fiery Oven. "Give an account of your rule in the face of those whom you provoked to mischief," He said to Satan. "My balance hitched to a beam will weigh the good and evil of my children, and if good is heavier than evil, I shall lighten your countenance and clothe you with the robes of angels."

"Awake the dead" He bade the Trumpeter, and "Lift the lids off the burying-places" He bade the labourers. In their generations were they called; "for," said the Lord, "good and evil are customs of a period and when the period is passed and the next is come, good may be evil and evil may be good."

Now God did not put His entire trust in Satan, and in the evening of the day He set to prove him:

"It is over."

"My Lord, so be it," answered Satan.

"How now?" asked God.

"The scale of wickedness sways like a kite in the wind," cried Satan. "Give me my robes and I will transgress against you no more."

"In the Book of Heaven and Hell," said God, "there is no writing of the last of the Welsh."

Satan spoke up: "My Lord, your pledge concerned those judged on the Day of Judgment. Day is outing. The windows of the Mansion are lit; hark the angels tuning their golden strings for the cheer of the Resurrection Supper. Give me my robes that I may sing your praises."

"Can I not lengthen the day with a wink of my eye?"

"All things you can do, my Lord, but observe your pledge to me. Allow these people to rest a while longer. Their number together with the number of their sins is fewer than the hairs on Elisha's head."

God laughed in His heart as He replied to Satan: "Tell the Trumpeter to take his horn and the labourers their spades and bring to me the Welsh."

The labourers digged, and at the sound of the horn the dead breathed and heaved. Those whose wit was sharp hurried into neighbouring chapels and stole Bibles and hymn-books, with which in their pockets and under their arms they joined the host in Heaven's Courtyard, whence they went into the Waiting Chamber that is without the Judgment Hall.

"Boy bach, a lot of Books of the Word he has," a woman remarked to the Respected Towy-

Watkins. "Say him I have one."

"Happy would I be to do like that," was the reply. "But, female, much does the Large One regard His speeches. What is the text on the wall? 'Prepare your deeds for the Lord.' The Beybile is the most religious deed. Farewell for now," and he pretended to go away.

Holding the sleeve of his White Shirt, the woman separated her toothless gums and fashioned her wrinkled face in grief. "Two tens he has," she croaked. "And his shirt is clean. Dirty am I; buried I was as I was found, and the shovellers beat the soil through the top of the coffin. Do much will I for one Beybile."

"A poor dab you are," said Towy. "Many deeds you have? But no odds to me."

"Four I have."

"Woe for you, unfortunate."

"Iss-iss, horrid is my plight," the woman whined. "Little I did for Him."

"Don't draw tears. For eternity you'll weep. Here is a massive Beybile for your four deeds."

"Take him one. Handy will three be in the minute of the questioning."

"Refusing the Beybile bach you are. Also the hymn-book — old and new notations — I present for four. Stupid am I as the pigger's prentice who bought the litter in the belly."

"Be him soft and sell for one."

"I cannot say less. No relation you are to me. Hope I do that right enough are your four. Recite them to me, old woman."

"I ate rats to provide a Beybile to the

Respected," the woman trembled. "I——"

"You are pathetic," Towy said. "Hie and get your tokens and have that poor one will I because of my pity for you."

The woman told her deeds in Heaven's Record Office, and she was given four white tablets on which her deeds were inscribed; and the rat tablet Towy took from her. "Faith and hope are tidy heifers," he said, "but a stallion is charity. Priceless Beybile I give you, sinner."

As he moved away Towy cried in the manner of one selling by auction: "This is the beloved Beybile of Jesus. This is the book of hymns — old and new notations. Hymns harvest, communion, funerals, Sunday schools, and hymns for children bach are here. Treasures bulky for certain."

For some he received three tablets each, for some five tablets each, and for some ten tablets each. But the gaudy Bible which was decorated with pictures and ornamented with brass clasps and a leather covering he did not sell; nor did he sell the gilt-edged hymn-book. Between the leaves of his Bible he put his tablets — as a preacher his markers — the writing on each tablet confirming a verse in the place it was set. His labour over, he chanted: "Pen Calvaria! Pen Calvaria! Very soon will come to view." Men and women gazed upon him, envying him; and those who had Bibles and hymn-books hastened to do as he had done.

Among the many that came to him was one whose name was Ben Lloyd.

"Dear me," said Towy.

"Dear me," said Ben.

"Fat is my religion after the springing," cried Towy. "Perished was I and up again. Amen, Big Man. Amen and amen. And amen."

"I opened my eyes and I saw a hand thrusting aside the firmament and I heard One calling me from the beyond, and the One was God."

"Like the roar of heated bulls was the noise, Ben bach."

"Praise Him I did that I was laid to rest at home. Apart from the stir of Parliament. Tell Him I will how my spirit, though the flesh was dead, bathed in the living rivers and walked in the peaceful valleys of the glorious land of my fathers — thinking, thinking of Jesus."

"Hold on. Not so fast. From Capel Bryn Salem I journeyed to mouth with my heart to the Lord, and your slut of a widow paid me only four soferens. Eloquent sermon I spouted and four soferens is the price of a supply."

"In your charity forgive her; her sorrow was overpowering."

"Sorrow! The mule of an English! She wasn't there."

"You don't say," cried Ben. " If above she is I will have her dragged down."

"Not a stone did she put over your head, and the strumpets of your sisters did not tend your grave. Why you were not eaten by worms I can't know."

On a sudden Towy shouted: "See an old parson do I. Is not this the day of rising up? Awful if the Big Man mistakes us for the Church. Not been inside a church have I, drop dead and blind, since I was born."

None gave heed to his cry, for the sound of the bargaining was most high. "Dissenters," he bellowed, "what right have Church heathens to mix with us? The Fiery Oven is their home."

The people were dismayed. Their number being small, the Church folk were pressed one upon the other; and after they were thrown in a mass against the gate of the Chariot House the Dissenters spread themselves easily as far as the door of the Crooked Stairway.

"Now, boys capel," Towy-Watkins said, "we will have a sermon. Fine will Welsh be in the nostrils of the Big Preacher. Pray will I at once."

The prayer ended, and one struck his tuning-fork; and while the congregation moaned and lamented, a tall man, who wore the habit of a preacher and whose yellow beard — the fringe of which was singed — hung over his breast like a sheaf of wheat, passed through the way of the door of the Stairway, and as he walked towards the Judgment Hall, some said: "Fair day, Respected," and some said: "Similar he is to Towy-Watkins."

"Shut your throats, colts," Towy rebuked the people. "Say after me: 'Go round my backhead, Satan.'"

"Go round my backhead, Satan," the people obeyed.

"Catch him and skin him," Towy screamed. "Teach him we will to snook about here."

Fear arming his courage, Satan shouted: "He who hurts me him shall I pitch headlong to the flames." The people's hands went to their sides, and Satan departed in peace.

"In my heart is my head," Towy said. "Near the Oven we are. Blow your noses of the stench. Young youths, herd blockheads Church over here."

Before the stalwarts started on their errand, the Overseer of the Waiting Chamber came to the door of the lane that takes you into the Judgment Hall, wherefore the Dissenters wept, howled, and whooped.

"Ready am I, God bach," Towy exclaimed, stretching his hairy arms. "Take me."

"Patiently I waited for the last Trump and humbly do I now wait for the Crown from your fingers," said Ben Lloyd. "My deeds are recorded in the archives of the House of Commons and the Cymmrodorion Society."

"Clap up," Towy admonished Ben. "My religious actions can't be counted."

Lowering his eyes the Overseer murmured: "I am not the Lord."

"For why did you not say that?" cried Towy. He stepped to the Overseer. "Hap you are Apostle Shames. A splendid photo of Shames is in the Beybile with pictures. Fond am I of preaching from him. Lovely pieces there are. 'Abram believed God'. Who was Abram? Father of Isaac bach. Who made Abram? The Big Man. And the Big Man made the capel and the respected that is the jewel of the capel. Is not the pulpit the throne? Glad am I to see you, indeed, Shames."

The Overseer opened his lips.

"Enter with you will I," said Towy. "Look through my glassy soul you can."

"Silence——" the Overseer began.

"Iss, silence for ever and ever, amen," said Towy. "No trial I need. How can the Judge judge if there's no judging to be? Go up will I then. Hope to see you again, Shames."

The Overseer tightened his girdle. "Thus saith the Lord," he proclaimed: "'I will consider each by his deeds or all by the deeds of their two apostles.'"

"Ho-ho," said Towy. "Half one moment. Think will we. Dissenters, crowd here. Ben Lloyd, make arguments. Tricky is old Shames."

The Dissenters assembled close to Ben and Towy, and the Church people crept near them in order to share their counsel; but the Dissenters turned upon their enemies and bruised them with fists and Bibles and hymn-books, and called them frogs, turks, thieves, atheists, blacks; and there never has been heard such a tumult in any house. Alarmed that he could not part one side from the other, the Overseer sought Satan, who had a name for crafty dealings with disputants.

Satan was distressed. "If it was not for personal reasons," he said, "I would let them go to Hell." He sent into the Chamber a carpenter who put a barrier from wall to wall, and he appointed Jude in charge of the barrier to guard that no one went under it or over it.

Then the wise men of the Dissenters continued to examine the Lord's offer; and a thousand men declared they were holy enough to go before God, and from the thousand five hundred were cast out, and from the five hundred three hundred, and from the two hundred one hundred were cast away. Now this hundred were Baptists, Methodists, and

Congregationalists, and they quarrelled so harshly and decried one another so spitefully that Ben and Towy made with them a compact to speak specially for each of them in the private ear of God. The strife quelled and Towy having cried loudly: "Dissenters and Churchers, glad you are that me and Ben Lloyd, Hem Pee, are your apostles," he and Ben followed the Overseer.

In the Judgment Hall the two apostles crouched to pray, and they were stirred by Satan laying his hands on their shoulders.

"Prayers are useless here, my friends," said the Devil. "We must proceed with the business. I am just as anxious as you are that everything reaches a satisfactory conclusion."

"I object," said Ben. "Solemnly object. I don't know this infidel. I don't want to know him."

"Go from here," Towy gruntled. "A sweat is in my whiskers. Inhabitants, why isn't his tongue a red-hot poker?... Well, boys Palace, grand this is. Say who you are?" he asked one whose face shone like a mirror. "Respected Towy-Watkins am I."

He whose face shone like a polished mirror answered that he was Moses the Keeper of the Balance. "The Lord is in the Cloud," he said.

Towy addressed the Cloud, which was the breadth of a man's hand, and which was brighter than the golden halo of the throne: "Big Man, peep at your helper. Was not I a ruler over the capel? Religious were my prayers."

"I did not hear any," said God.

"Mistake. Mistake. Towy bach eloquent was I called. Here am I with the Speech, and the Speech

11

is God and God is the Speech. Take you as a great gift this nice hymn-book."

"What are hymns?" asked God.

"Moses, Moses," cried Towy, "explain affairs to Him."

God spoke: "Satan, render your account of the mischief you made these men do."

"This is a travesty of the traditions of the House," said Ben. "Traditions that are dear to me, being taught them at my mother's knees. I refuse to be drenched in Satan's froth. Against one who was a member of the Government you are taking the evidence of the most discredited man in the universe — the world's worst sinner."

He ceased, because Satan had begun to read; and Satan read rapidly, with shame, and without pantomime, not pausing at what times he was abused and charged with lying; and he read correctly, for the Records Clerk followed him word by word in the Book of the Watchers; and for every sin to which he confessed Moses placed a scarlet tablet in the scale of wickedness.

"I will attend to what I have heard," said the Lord when Satan had finished. "Put your tablets in the scale and go into the Chamber."

Ben and Towy withdrew, and as they passed out they beheld that the scale of scarlet tablets touched the ground.

Then the Cloud vanished and God came out of the Cloud.

"My wrath is fierce," He said. "Bind these Welsh and torment them with vipers and with fire in the uttermost parts of Hell. They shall have no more remembrance before me."

"Will you destroy the just?" asked Moses.

"They have chosen."

"Shall the godly perish because of the god-less?"

"I flooded the world," said God.

"The righteous Noah and his house and his animals you did not destroy. And you repented that you smote every living thing. May not my Lord repent again?"

"I am not destroying every living thing," God replied. "I am destroying the vile."

"Remember Sodom and Gomorrah, Lot's wife and his daughters. They all sinned after their deliverance. The doings of Sodom stayed."

Moses also said: "You gave your ear to Jonah from the well of the sea."

"I sacrificed my Son for man."

"And loosed Satan upon him."

"Is scarlet white?" asked God.

"Is justice the fruit of injustice? The two men were not of the Church, and the Church may be holy in your sight."

"I have judged."

"And your judgment is past understanding," said Moses, and he sat at the Balance.

The servants of the Lord spoke one with another: "I cannot eat of the supper," said one; "The songs will be as a wolf's howlings in the wilderness," said another; "The honey will be as bitter-sweet as Adam's apple," said a third. But Satan exclaimed: "Come, let us seek in the Book of the Watchers for an act that will turn Him from His purpose."

In seeking, some put their fingers on the leaves and advised Moses to cry unto the Lord in such and such a manner.

"My voice is dumb," replied Moses.

Satan presently astonished the servants; he took the book to the Lord. "My Lord," he said, "which is the more precious — good or evil? "

"Good," said the Lord.

"More precious than the riches of Solomon is a deed done in your name?"

"Yes."

"Though the sins were as numerous as the teeth of a shoal of fish?"

"So. Unravel your riddle."

"An old woman of the Dissenters," said Satan, "claimed four tablets, whereas her deeds were nine."

God looked at the Balance and lo, the scale of white tablets was heavier than the scale of scarlet tablets.

"Bid hither the apostles," He commanded the Overseer, "for they shall see me, and this day they and their flocks shall be in Paradise."

Satan stood before the face of Moses, glowing as the angels; and he brought out scissors to clip off the fringe of his beard. When he had cut only a little, the Overseer entered the Judgment Hall, saying: "The two apostles tricked Jude and crawled under the barrier, and they shot back the bolts of the gate of the Chariot House and called a charioteer to take them to Heaven. 'This is God's will,' they said to him."

Satan's scissors fell on the floor.

ACCORDING TO THE PATTERN

# ACCORDING TO THE PATTERN

ON the eve of a Communion Sunday Simon Idiot espied Dull Anna washing her feet in the spume on the shore; he came out of his hiding-place and spoke jestingly to Anna and enticed her into Blind Cave, where he had sport with her. In the ninth year of her child, whom she had called Abel, Anna stretched out her tongue at the schoolmaster and took her son to the man who farmed Deinol.

"Brought have I your scarecrow," she said. "Give you to me the brown pennies that you will pay for him."

From dawn to sunset Abel stood on a hedge, waving his arms, shouting, and mimicking the sound of gunning. Weary of his work he vowed a vow that he would not keep on at it. He walked to Morfa and into his mother's cottage; his mother listened to him, then she took a stick and beat him until he could not rest nor move with ease.

"Break him in like a frisky colt, little man bach," said Anna to the farmer. "Know you he is the son of Satan. Have I not told how the Bad Man came to me in my sound sleep and was naughty with me?"

But the farmer had compassion on Abel and dealt with him kindly, and when Abel married he let him live in Tybach — the mud-walled, straw-

17

thatched, two-roomed house which is midway on the hill that goes down from Synod Inn into Morfa — and he let him farm six acres of land.

The young man and his bride so laboured that the people thereabout were confounded; they stirred earlier and lay down later than any honest folk; and they took more eggs and tubs of butter to market than even Deinol, and their pigs fattened wondrously quick.

Twelve years did they live thus wise. For the woman these were years of toil and child-bearing; after she had borne seven daughters, her sap husked and dried up.

Now the spell of Abel's mourning was one of ill-fortune for Deinol, the master of which was grown careless: hay rotted before it was gathered and corn before it was reaped, potatoes were smitten by a blight, a disease fell upon two cart-horses, and a heifer was drowned in the sea. Then the farmer felt embittered, and by day and night he drank himself drunk in the inns of Morfa.

Because he wanted Deinol, Abel brightened himself up: he wore whipcord leggings over his short legs, and a preacher's coat over his long trunk, a white and red patterned celluloid collar about his neck, and a bowler hat on the back of his head; and his side-whiskers were trimmed in the shape of a spade. He had joy of many widows and spinsters, to each of whom he said: "There's a grief-livener you are," and all of whom he gave over on hearing of the widow of Drefach. Her he married, and with the money he got with her, and the money he borrowed, he bought Deinol. Soon he was freed from the hands of his lender. He had eight horses and twelve cows, and he had oxen and heifers, and pigs and hens, and he had twenty-five sheep grazing on his moorland. As his birth and poverty had caused him to be scorned, so now his gains caused him to be respected. The preacher of Capel Dissenters in Morfa saluted him on the tramping road and in shop, and brought him down from the gallery to the Big Seat. Even if Abel had land, money, and honour his vessel of contentment was not filled until his wife went into her deathbed and gave him a son.

"Indeed me," he cried, "Benshamin his name shall be. The Large Maker gives and a One He is for taking away."

He composed a prayer of thankfulness and of sorrow; and this prayer he recited to the congregation which gathered at the graveside of the woman from Drefach.

Benshamin grew up in the way of Capel Dissenters. He slept with his father and ate apart from his sisters, for his mien was lofty. At the age of seven he knew every question and answer in the book "Mother's Gift," with sayings from which he scourged sinners; and at the age of eight he delivered from memory the Book of Job at the Seiet; at that age also he was put among the elders in the Sabbath School.

He advanced, waxing great in religion. On the nights of the Saying and Searching of the Word he was with the cunningest men, disputing with the preacher, stressing his arguments with his fingers, and proving his learning with phrases from the sermons of the saintly Shones Talysarn.

19

If one asked him: "What are you going, Ben Abel Deinol?" he always answered: "The errander of the White Gospel fach."

His father communed with the preacher, who said: "Pity quite sinful if the boy is not in the pulpit."

"Like that do I think as well too," replied Abel. "Eloquent he is. Grand he is spouting prayers at his bed. Weep do I."

Neighbours neglected their fields and barnyards to hear the lad's shoutings to God. Once Ben opened his eyes and rebuked those who were outside his room.

"Shamed you are, not for certain," he said to them. "Come in, boys Capel. Right you hear the Gospel fach. Youngish am I but old is my courtship of King Jesus who died on the tree for scamps of parsons."

He shut his eyes and sang of blood, wood, white shirts, and thorns; of the throng that would arise from the burial-ground, in which there were more graves than molehills in the shire. He cried against the heathenism of the Church, the wickedness of Church tithes, and against ungodly bookprayers and short sermons.

Early Ben entered College Carmarthen, where his piety — which was an adage — was above that of any student. Of him this was said: "White Jesus bach is as plain on his lips as the purse of a big bull."

Brightness fell upon him. He had a name for the tearfulness and splendour of his eloquence. He could conduct himself fancifully: now he was

Pharoah wincing under the plagues, now he was the Prodigal Son longing to eat at the pigs' trough, now he was the Widow of Nain rejoicing at the recovery of her son, now he was a parson in Nineveh squirming under the prophecy of Jonah; and his hearers winced or longed, rejoiced or squirmed. Congregations sought him to preach in their pulpits, and he chose such as offered the highest reward, pledging the richest men for his wage and the cost of his entertainment and journey. But Ben would rule over no chapel. "I wait for the call from above," he said.

His term at Carmarthen at an end, he came to Deinol. His father met him dolefully.

"An old boy very cruel is the Parson," Abel whined. "Has he not strained Gwen for his tithes? Auction her he did and bought her himself for three pounds and half a pound."

Ben answered: "Go now and say the next Saturday Benshamin Lloyd will give mouthings on tithes in Capel Dissenters."

Ben stood in the pulpit, and he spoke to the people of Capel Dissenters.

"How many of you have been to his church?" he cried. "Not one male bach or one female fach. Go there the next Sabbath, and the black muless will not say to you: 'Welcome you are, persons Capel. But there's glad am I to see you.' A comic sermon you will hear. A sermon got with half-a-crown postal order. Ask Postman. Laugh highly you will and stamp on the floor. Funny is the Parson in the white frock. Ach y fy, why for he doesn't have a coat preacher like Respecteds? Ask me that. From

21

where does his Church come from? She is the inheritance of Satan. The only thing he had to leave, and he left her to his friends the parsons. Iss-iss, earnest affair is this. Who gives him his food? We. Who pays for Vicarage? We. Who feeds his pony? We. His cows? We. Who built his church? We. With stones carted from our quarries and mortar messed about with the tears of our mothers and the blood of our fathers."

At the gate of the chapel men discussed Ben's words; and two or three of them stole away and herded Gwen into the corner of the field; and they caught her and cut off her tail, and drove a staple into her udder. Sunday morning eleven men from Capel Dissenters, with iron bands to their clogs on their feet, and white aprons before their bellies, shouted without the church: "We are come to pray from the book." The parson was affrighted, and left over tolling his bell, and he bolted and locked the door, against which he set his body as one would set the stub of a tree.

Running at the top of their speed the railers came to Ben, telling how the Parson had put them to shame.

"Iobs you are," Ben answered. "The boy bach who loses the key of his house breaks into his house. Does an old wench bar the dairy to her mishtress?"

The men returned each to his abode, and an hour after midday they gathered in the church burial-ground, and they drew up a tombstone, and with it rammed the door; and they hurled stones at the windows; and in the darkness they built a wall of dung in the room of the door.

Repentance sank into the parson as he saw and remembered that which had been done to him. He called to him his servant Lissi Workhouse, and her he told to take Gwen to Deinol. The cow lowed woefully as she was driven; she was heard even in Morfa, and many hurried to the road to witness her. Abel was at the going in of the close.

"Well-well, Lissi Workhouse," he said, "what's doing then?"

"'Go give the male his beast,' mishtir talked."

"Right for you are," said Abel. "Right for enough is the rascal. But a creature without blemish he pilfered. Hit her and hie her off."

As Lissi was about to go, Ben cried from within the house: "The cow the fulbert had was worth two of his cows."

"Sure, iss-iss," said Abel. "Go will I to Vicarage with boys capel. Bring the baston, Ben bach."

Ben came out, and his ardour warmed up on beholding Lissi's broad hips, scarlet cheeks, white teeth, and full bosoms.

"Not blaming you, girl fach, am I," he said. "My father, journey with Gwen. Walk will I with Lissi Workhouse."

That afternoon Abel brought a cow in calf into his close; and that night Ben crossed the mown hay-fields to the Vicarage, and he threw a little gravel at Lissi's window.

\*     \*     \*

23

The hay was gathered and stacked and thatched, and the corn was cut down, and to the women who were gleaning his father's oats, Ben said how that Lissi was in the family way.

"Silence your tone, indeed," cried one, laughing. "No sign have I seen."

"If I die," observed a large woman, "boy bach pretty innocent you are, Benshamin. Four months have I yet. And not showing much do I."

"No," said another, "the bulk might be only the coil of your apron, ho-ho."

"Whisper to us," asked the large woman, "who the foxer is. Keep the news will we."

"Who but the scamp of the Parson?" replied Ben. "What a sow of a hen."

By such means Ben shifted his offence. On being charged by the Parson he rushed through the roads crying that the enemy of the Big Man had put unbecoming words on a harlot's tongue. Capel Dissenters believed him. "He could not act wrongly with a sheep," some said.

So Ben tasted the sapidness and relish of power, and his desires increased.

"Mortgage Deinol, my father bach," he said to Abel. "Going am I to London. Heavy shall I be there. None of the dirty English are like me."

"Already have I borrowed for your college. No more do I want to have. How if I sell a horse?"

"Sell you the horse too, my father bach."

"Done much have I for you," Abel said. "Fairish I must be with your sisters."

"Why for you cavil like that, father? The money of mam came to Deinol. Am I not her son?"

Though his daughters murmured — "We wake at the caw of the crows," they said, "and weary in the young of the day" — Abel obeyed his son, who thereupon departed and came to Thornton East to the house of Catherine Jenkins, a widow woman, with whom he took the appearance of a burning lover.

Though he preached with a view at many English chapels in London, none called him. He caused Abel to sell cattle and mortgage Deinol for what it was worth and to give him all the money he received therefrom; he swore such hot love for Catherine that the woman pawned her furniture for his sake.

Intrigued that such scant fruit had come up from his sowings, Ben thought of further ways of stablishing himself. He inquired into the welfare of shop assistants from women and girls who worshipped in Welsh chapels, and though he spoiled several in his quest, the abominations which oppressed these workers were made known to him. Shop assistants carried abroad his fame and called him "Fiery Taffy." Ben showed them how to rid themselves of their burden; "a burden," he said, "packed full and overflowing by men of my race — the London Welsh drapers."

The Welsh drapers were alarmed and in a rage with Ben. They took the opinion of their big men and performed slyly. Enos-Harries — this is the Enos-Harries who has a drapery shop in Kingsend — sent to Ben this letter: "Take Dinner with Slf and Wife same, is Late Dinner I am pleased to inform. You we don't live in Establishment only as per printed Note Heading. And Oblige."

Enos-Harries showed Ben his house, and told him the cost of the treasures that were therein.

Also Harries said: "I have learned of you as a promising Welshman, and I want to do a good turn for you with a speech by you on St David's Day at Queen's Hall. Now, then."

"I am not important enough for that."

"She'll be a first-class miting in tip-top speeches. All the drapers and dairies shall be there in crowds. Three sirs shall come."

"I am choked with engagements," said Ben. "I am preaching very busy now just."

"Well-well. Asked I did for you are a clean Cymro bach. As I repeat, only leading lines in speakers shall be there. Come now into the drawing-room and I'll give you an intro to the Missus Enos-Harries. In evening dress she is — chik Paris Model. The invoice price was ten-ten."

"Wait a bit," Ben remarked. " I would be glad if I could speak."

"Perhaps the next time we give you the invite. The Cymmrodorion shall be in the miting."

"As you plead, try I will."

"Stretching a point am I," Harries said. "This is a favour for you to address this glorious miting where the Welsh drapers will attend and the Missus Enos-Harries will sing 'Land of my Fathers'."

Ben withdrew from his fellows for three days, and on the third day — which was that of the Saint — he put on him a frock coat, and combed down his moustache over the blood-red swelling on his lip; and he cleaned his teeth. Here are some of the sayings that he spoke that night:

"Half an hour ago we were privileged to listen to the voice of a lovely lady — a voice as clear as a diamond ring. It inspired us one and all with a hiraeth for the dear old homeland — for dear Wales, for the land of our fathers and mothers too, for the land that is our heritage not by Act of Parliament but by the Act of God....

"Who ownss this land to-day? The squaire and the parshon. By what right? By the same right as the thief who steals your silk and your laces, and your milk and butter, and your reddy-made blousis. I know a farm of one hundred acres, each rod having been tamed from heatherland into a manna of abundance. Tamed by human bones and muscles — God's invested capital in His chosen children. Six months ago this land — this fertile and rich land — was wrestled away from the owners. The bones of the living and the dead were wrestled away. I saw it three months ago — a wylderness. The clod had been squeesed of its zweat. The land belonged to my father, and his father, and his father, back to countless generations....

"I am proud to be among my people tonight. How sorry I am for anyone who are not Welsh. We have a language as ancient as the hills that shelter us, and the rivers that never weery of refreshing us....

"Only recently a few shop assistants — a handful of counter-jumpers — tried to shake the integrity of our commerse. But their white cuffs held back their aarms, and the white collars choked their aambitions. When I was a small boy my mam used to tell me how the chief Satan was caught trying to put his hand over the sun so as to give other satans a chance of doing wrong on earth in the dark. That was the object of these misguided fools. They had no grievances. I have since investigated the questions of living-in and fines. Both are fair and necessary. The man who tries to destroy them is like the swimmer who plunges among the water lilies to be dragged into destruction....

"Welsh was talked in the Garden of Aden. That is where commerse began. Didn't Eve buy the apple?...

"Ladies and gentlemen, Cymmrodorion, listen. There is a going in these classical old rafterss. It is the coming of God. And the message He gives you this night is this: 'Men of Gwalia, march on and keep you tails up.'"

From that hour Ben flourished. He broke his league with the shop assistants. Those whom he had troubled lost courage and humbled themselves before their employers; but their employers would have none of them, man or woman, boy or girl.

Vexation followed his prosperity. His father reproached him, writing: "Sad I drop into the Pool as old Abel Tybach, and not as Lloyd Deinol." Catherine harassed him to recover her house and chattels. To these complainings he was deaf. He married the daughter of a wealthy Englishman, who set him up in a large house in the midst of a pleasure garden; and of the fatness and redness of his wife he was sickened before he was wedded to her.

By studying diligently, the English language became nearly as familiar to him as the Welsh language. He bound himself to Welsh politicians and engaged himself in public affairs, and soon he was as an idol to a multitude of people, who were sensible only to his well-sung words, and who did not know that his utterances veiled his own avarice and that of his masters. All that he did was for profit, and yet he could not win enough.

Men and women, soothed into false ease and quickened into counterfeit wrath, commended him, crying: "Thank God for Ben Lloyd." Such praise puffed him up, and howsoever mighty he was in the view of fools, he was mightier in his own view.

"At the next election I'll be in Parliament," he boasted in his vanity. "The basis of my solidity — strength — is as immovable — is as impregnable as Birds' Rock in Morfa."

Though the grandson of Simon Idiot and Dull Anna prophesied great things for himself, it was evil that came to him.

He trembled from head to foot to ravish every comely woman on whom his ogling eyes dwelt. His greed made him faithless to those whom he professed to serve: in his eagerness to lift himself he planned, plotted, and trafficked with the foes of his officers. Hearing that an account of his misdeeds was spoken abroad, he called the high London Welshmen into a room, and he said to them:

"These cruel slanderers have all but broken my spirit. They are the wicked inventions of fiends incarnate. It is not my fall that is required — if that were so I would gladly make the sacrifise — the zupreme sacrifise, if wanted — but it is the fall of the Party that these men are after. He who repeats one foul thing is doing his level best to destroy the fabric of this magnificent organisation that has been reared by your brains. It has no walls of stone and mortar, yet it is a sity builded by men. We must have no more bickerings. We have work to do. The seeds are springing forth, and a goodly harvest is promised: let us sharpen our blades and clear our barn floors. Cymru Fydd — Wales for the Welsh — is here. At home and at Westminster our kith and kin are occupying prominent positions. Disestablishment is at hand. We have closed public houses and erected chapels, each chapel being a factor in the education of the masses in ideas of righteous government. You, my friends, have secured much of the land, around which you have made walls, and in which you have set water fountains, and have planted rare plants and flowers. And you have put up your warning signs on it — 'Trespassers will be prosecuted.'

"There is coming the Registration of Workers Act, by which every worker will be held to his locality, to his own enormous advantage. And it will end strikes, and trades unionism will deservedly crumble. In future these men will be able to settle down, and with God's blessing bring children into the world, and their condition will be a delight unto themselves and a profit to the community.

"But we must do more. I must do more. And you must help me. We must stand together. Slander never creates; it shackles and kills. We must be solid. Midway off the Cardigan coast — in beautiful Morfa — there is a rock — Birds' Rock. As a boy I used to climb to the top of it, and watch the waters swirling and tumbling about it, and around it and against it. But I was unafraid. For I knew that the rock was old when man was young, and that it had braved all the washings of the sea."

The men congratulated Ben; and Ben came home and he stood at a mirror, and shaping his body put out his arms.

"How's this for my maiden speech in the House?" he asked his wife. Presently he paused. "You're a fine one to be an M.P.'s lady," he said. "You stout, underworked fool."

Ben urged on his imaginings: he advised his monarch, and to him for favours merchants brought their gold, and mothers their daughters. Winter and spring moved, and then his mind brought his enemies to his door.

"As the root of a tree spreads in the bosom of the earth," he said, "so my fame shall spread over the world"; and he built a fence about his house.

But his mind would not be stilled. Every midnight his enemies were at the fence, and he could not sleep for the dreadful outcry; every midnight he arose from his bed and walked aside the fence, testing the strength of it with a hand and a shoulder and shooing away his enemies as one does a brood of chickens from a cornfield.

His fortieth summer ran out — a season of short days and nights speeding on the heels of night. Then peace fell upon him; and at dusk of a day he came into his room, and he saw one sitting in a chair. He went up to the chair and knelt on a knee, and said: "Your Majesty..."

EARTHBRED

# EARTHBRED

BECAUSE he was diseased with a consumption, Evan Roberts in his thirtieth year left over being a drapery assistant and had himself hired as a milk roundsman.

A few weeks thereafter he said to Mary, the woman whom he had promised to wed: "How now if I had a milk shop?"

Mary encouraged him, and searched for that which he desired; and it came to be that on a Thursday afternoon they two met at the mouth of Worship Street — the narrow lane that is at the going into Richmond. "Stand here, Marri," Evan ordered. "Go in will I and have words with the owner. Hap I shall uncover his tricks."

"Very well you are," said Mary. "Don't over-waggle your tongue. Address him in hidden phrases."

Evan entered the shop, and as there was no one therein he made an account of the tea packets and flour bags which were on the shelves. Presently a small, fat woman stood beyond the counter. Evan addressed her in English: "Are you Welsh?"

"That's what people say," the woman answered.

"Glad am I to hear you," Evan returned in Welsh. "Tell me how you was."

"A Cymro bach I see," the woman cried. "How was you?"

"Peeped did I on your name on the sign. Shall I say you are Mistress Jinkins?"

"Iss, indeed, man."

"What about affairs these close days?"

"Busy we are. Why for you ask? Trade you do in milk?"

"Blurt did I for nothing," Evan replied.

"No odds, little man. Ach y fy, jealous other milkmen are of us. There's nasty some people are."

"Natty shop you have. Little shop and big traffic, Mistress Jinkins?"

"Quick you are."

"Know you Tom Mathias Tabernacle Street?" Evan inquired.

"Seen him have I in the big meetings at Capel King's Cross."

"Getting on he is, for certain sure. Hundreds of pints he sells. And groceries."

"Pwf," Mrs Jenkins sneered. "Fulbert you are to believe him. A liar without shame is Twm. And a cheat. Bad sampler he is of the Welsh."

"Speak I do as I hear. More thriving is your concern."

"No boast is in me. But don't we do thirty gallons?"

Evan summoned up surprise into his face, and joy. "Dear me to goodness," he exclaimed. "Take something must I now. Sell you me an egg."

Evan shook the egg at his ear. "She is good," he remarked.

"Weakish is the male," observed Mrs Jenkins. "Much trouble he has in his inside."

"Poor bach," replied Evan. "Well-well. Fair

night for today."

"Why for you are in a hurry?"

"Woman fach, for what you do not know that I abide in Wandsworth and the clock is late?"

Mrs Jenkins laughed. "Boy pretty sly you are. Come you to Richmond to buy one egg?" Evan coughed and spat upon the ground, and while he cleaned away his spittle with a foot he said: "Courting business have I on the Thursdays. The wench is in a shop draper."

"How shall I mouth where she is? With Wright?"

"In shop Breach she is." He spoke this in English: "So long."

In that language also did Mrs Jenkins answer him: "Now we shan't be long."

Narrowing his eyes and crooking his knees, Evan stood before Mary. "Like to find out more would I," he said. "Guess did the old female that I had seen the adfertissment."

"Blockhead you are to bare your mind," Mary admonished him.

"Why for you call me blockhead when there's no blockhead to be?"

"Sorry am I, dear heart. But do you hurry to marry me. You know that things are so and so. The month has shown nothing."

"Shut your head, or I'll change my think altogether."

The next week Evan called at the dairy shop again.

"How was the people?" he cried on the threshold.

Mrs Jenkins opened the window which was at

the back of her, and called out: "The boy from Wales is here, Dai."

Stooping as he moved through the way of the door, Dai greeted Evan civilly: "How was you this day?"

"Quite grand," Evan answered.

"What capel do you go?"

"Walham Green, dear man."

"Good preach there was by the Respected Eynon Daviss the last Sabbath morning, shall I ask? Eloquent is Eynon."

"In the night do I go."

"Solemn serious, go you ought in the mornings."

"Proper is your saying," Evan agreed. "Perform I would if I could."

"Biggish is your round, perhaps?" said Dai.

"Iss-iss. No-no." Evan was confused.

Don't be afraid of your work. Crafty is your manner."

Evan had not anything to say.

"Fortune there is in milk," said Dai. "Study you the size of her. Little she is. Heavy will be my loss. The rent is only fifteen bob a week. And thirty gallons and more do I do. Broke is my health," and Dai laid the palms of his hands on his belly and groaned.

"Here he is to visit his wench," said Mrs Jenkins.

"You're not married now just?" asked Dai.

"Better in his pockets trousers is a male for a woman," said Mrs Jenkins.

"Comforting in your pockets trousers is a

woman," Dai cried.

"Clap your throat," said Mrs Jenkins. "Redness you bring to my skin."

Evan retired and considered.

"Tempting is the business," he told Mary. "Fancy do I to know more of her. Come must I still once yet."

"Be not slothful," Mary pleaded. "Already I feel pains, and quickly the months pass."

Then Evan charged her to watch over the shop, and to take a count of the people who went into it. So Mary walked in the street. Mrs Jenkins saw her and imagined her purpose, and after she had proved her, she and Dai formed a plot whereby many little children and young youths and girls came into the shop. Mary numbered everyone, but the number that she gave Evan was three times higher than the proper number. The man was pleased, and he spoke out to Dai. "Tell me the price of the shop," he said.

"Improved has the health," replied Dai. "And not selling I don't think am I."

"Pity that is. Great offer I have."

"Smother your cry. Taken a shop too have I in Petersham. Rachel will look after this."

Mrs Jenkins spoke to her husband with a low voice: "Witless you are. Let him speak figures."

"As you want if you like then," said Dai.

"A puzzle you demand this one minute," Evan murmured. "Thirty pounds would ——"

"Light is your head," Dai cried. "More than thirty gallons and a pram. Eighty I want for the shop and stock."

"I stop," Evan pronounced. "Thirty-five can I

give. No more and no less."

"Cute bargainer you are. Generous am I to give back five pounds for luck cash on spot. Much besides is my counter trade."

"Bring me papers for my eyes to see," said Evan.

Mrs Jenkins rebuked Evan: "Hoity-toity! Not Welsh you are. Old English boy."

"Tut-tut, Rachel fach," said Dai. "Right you are, and right and wrong is Evan Roberts. Books I should have. Trust I give and trust I take. I have no guile."

"How answer you to thirty-seven?" asked Evan.

"No more we've got, drop dead and blind."

He went away and related all to Mary.

"Lose the shop you will," Mary warned him. "And that's remorseful you'll be."

"Like this and that is the feeling," said Evan.

"Go to him," Mary counselled, "and say you will pay forty-five."

"No-no, foolish that is."

They two conferred with each other, and Mary gave to Evan all her money, which was almost twenty pounds; and Evan said to Dai: "I am not doubtful ——"

"Speak what is in you," Dai urged quickly.

"Test your shop will I for eight weeks as manager. I give you twenty down as earnest and twenty-five at the finish of the weeks if I buy her."

Dai and Rachel weighed that which Evan had proposed. The woman said: "A lawyer will do this"; the man said: "Splendid is the bargain and costly and thievish are old lawyers."

In this sort Dai answered Evan: "Do as you say. But I shall not give money for your work. Act you honestly by me. Did not mam carry me next my brother, who is a big preacher? Lend you will I a bed, and a dish or two and a plate, and a knife to eat food."

At this Mary's joy was abounding. "Put you up the banns," she said.

"Lots of days there is. Wait until I've bought the place."

Mary tightened her inner garments and loosened her outer garments, and every evening she came to the shop to prepare food for Evan, to make his bed, and to minister to him as a woman.

Now the daily custom at the shop was twelve gallons of milk, and the tea packets and flour bags which were on shelves were empty. Evan's anger was awful. He upbraided Mary, and he prayed to be shown how to worst Dai. His prayer was respected: at the end of the second week he gave Dai two pounds more than he had given him the week before.

"Brisk is trade," said Dai.

"I took into stock flour, tea, and four tins of job biscuits," replied Evan. "Am I not your servant?"

"Well done, good and faithful servant."

It was so that Evan bought more than he would sell, and each week he held a little money by fraud; and matches also and bundles of firewood and soap did he buy in Dai's name.

In the middle of the eighth week Dai came down to the shop.

"How goes it?" he asked in English.

"Fine, man. Fine." Changing his language, Evan said: "Keep her will I, and give you the money as I pledged. Take you the sum and sign you the paper bach."

Having acted accordingly, Dai cast his gaze on the shelves and on the floor, and he walked about judging aloud the value of what he saw: "Tea, three-pound-ten; biscuits, four-six; flour, four-five; fire-wood, five shillings; matches, one-ten; soap, one pound. Bring you these to Petersham. Put you them with the bed and the dishes I kindly lent you."

"For sure me, fulfil my pledge will I," Evan said.

He assembled Dai's belongings and placed them in a cart which he had borrowed; and on the back of the cart he hung a Chinese lantern which had in it a lighted candle. When he arrived at Dai's house, he cried: "Here is your ownings. Unload you them."

Dai examined the inside of the cart. "Mistake there is, Evan. Where's the stock?"

"Did I not pay you for your stock and shop? Forgetful you are."

Dai's wrath was such that neither could he blaspheme God nor invoke His help. Removing the slabber which was gathered in his beard and at his mouth, he shouted: "Put police on you will I."

"Away must I now," said Evan. "Come, take your bed."

"Not touch anything will I. Rachel, witness his roguery. Steal he does from the religious."

Evan drove off, and presently he became uneasy of the evil that might befall him were Dai

42

and Rachel to lay their hands on him; he led his horse into the unfamiliar and hard and steep road which goes up to the Star and Garter, and which therefrom falls into Richmond town. At what time he was at the top he heard the sound of Dai and Rachel running to him, each screaming upon him to stop. Rachel seized the bridle of the horse, and Dai tried to climb over the back of the cart. Evan bent forward and beat the woman with his whip, and she leaped aside. But Dai did not release his clutch, and because the lantern swayed before his face he flung it into the cart.

Evan did not hear any more voices, and misdeeming that he had got the better of his enemies, he turned, and, lo, the bed was in a yellow flame. He strengthened his legs and stretched out his thin upper lip, and pulled at the reins, saying: "Wo, now." But the animal thrust up its head and on a sudden galloped downwards. At the railing which divides two roads it was hindered, and Evan was thrown upon the ground. Men came forward to lift him, and he was dead.

FOR BETTER

# FOR BETTER

AT the time it was said of him "There's a boy that gets on he is," Enoch Harries was given Gwen the daughter of the builder Dan Thomas. On the first Sunday after her marriage the people of Kingsend Welsh Tabernacle crowded about Gwen, asking her: "How like you the bed, Messes Harries fach?" "Enoch has opened a shop butcher then?" "Any signs of a baban bach yet?" "Managed to get up quickly you did the day?" Gwen answered in the manner the questions were asked, seriously or jestingly. She considered these sayings, and the cause of her uneasiness was not a puzzle to her; and she got to despise the man whom she had married, and whose skin was like parched leather, and to repel his impotent embraces.

Withal she gave Enoch pleasure. She clothed herself with costly garments, adorned her person with rings and ornaments, and she modelled her hair in the way of a bob-wig. Enoch gave in to her in all things; he took her among Welsh master builders, drapers, grocers, dairymen, into their homes and such places as they assembled in; and his pride in his wife was nearly as great as his pride in the twenty plate-glass windows of his shop.

In her vanity Gwen exalted her estate.

"I hate living over the shop," she said. "It's so

common. Let's take a house away from here."

"Good that I am on the premizes," Enoch replied in Welsh. "Hap go wrong will affairs if I leave."

"We can't ask anyone decent here. Only commercials," Gwen said. With a show of care for her husband's welfare, she added: "Working too hard is my boy bach. And very splendid you should be."

Her design was fulfilled, and she and Enoch came to dwell in Thornton East, in a house near Richmond Park, and on the gate before the house, and on the door of the house, she put the name Windsor. From that hour she valued herself high. She had the words Mrs G. Enos-Harries printed on cards, and she did not speak of Enoch's trade in the hearing of anybody. She gave over conversing in Welsh, and would give no answer when spoken to in that tongue. She devised means continually to lift herself in the esteem of her neighbours, acting as she thought they acted: she had a man-servant and four maid-servants, and she instructed them to address her as the madam and Enoch as the master; she had a gong struck before meals and a bell rung during meals; the furniture in her rooms was as numerous as that in the windows of a shop; she went to the parish church on Sundays; she made feasts. But her life was bitter: tradespeople ate at her table and her neighbours disregarded her.

Enoch mollified her moaning with: "Never mind. I could buy the whole street up. I'll have you a motor car. Fine it will be with an advert on the front engine."

Still slighted, Gwen smoothed her misery with

deeds. She declared she was a Liberal, and she frequented Thornton Vale English Congregational Chapel. She gave ten guineas to the rebuilding fund, put a carpet on the floor of the pastor's parlour, sang at brotherhood gatherings, and entertained the pastor and his wife.

Wherefore her charity was discoursed thus: "Now when Peter spoke of a light that shines — shines, mark you — he was thinking of such ladies as Mrs G. Enos-Harries. Not forgetting Mr G. Enos-Harries."

"I'm going to build you a vestry," Gwen said to the pastor. "I'll organise a sale of work to begin with."

The vestry was set up, and Gwen bethought of one who should be charged with the opening ceremony of it, and to her mind came Ben Lloyd, whose repute was great among the London Welsh, and to whose house in Twickenham she rode in her car. Ben's wife answered her sharply: "He's awfully busy. And I know he won't see visitors."

"But won't you tell him? It will do him such a lot of good. You know what a stronghold of Toryism this place is."

A voice from an inner room cried: "Who is to see me?"

"Come this way," said Mrs Lloyd.

Ben, sitting at a table with writing paper and a Bible before him, rose.

"Messes Enos-Harries," he said, "long since I met you. No odds if I mouth Welsh? There's a language, dear me. This will not interest you in the least. Put your ambarelo in the cornel, Messes

Enos-Harries, and your backhead in a chair. Making a lecture am I."

Gwen told him the errand upon which she was bent, and while they two drank tea, Ben said: "Sing you a song, Messes Enos-Harries. Not forgotten have I your singing in Queen's Hall on the Day of David the Saint. Inspire me wonderfully you did with the speech. I've been sad too, but you are a wedded female. Sing you now then. Push your cup and saucer under the chair."

"No-no, not in tone am I," Gwen feigned.

"How about a Welsh hymn? Come in will I at the repeats."

"Messes Lloyd will sing the piano?"

"Go must she about her duties. She's a handless poor dab."

Gwen played and sang.

"Solemn pretty hymns have we," said Ben. "Are we not large?" He moved and stood under a picture which hung on the wall — his knees touching and his feet apart — and the picture was that of Cromwell. "My friends say I am Cromwell and Milton rolled into one. The Great Father gave me a child and He took him back to the Palace. Religious am I. Want I do to live my life in the hills and valleys of Wales: listening to the anthem of creation, and searching for Him under the bark of the tree. And there I shall wait for the sound of the last trumpet."

"A poet you are." Gwen was astonished.

"You are a poetess, for sure me," Ben said. He leaned over her. "Sparkling are your eyes. Deep brown are they — brown as the nut in the paws of the squirrel. Be you a bard and write about boys Cymru. Tell how they succeed in big London."

"I will try," said Gwen.

"Like you are and me. Think you do as I think."

"Know you for long I would," said Gwen.

"For ever," cried Ben. "But wedded you are. Read you a bit of the lecture will I." Having ended his reading and having sobbed over and praised that which he had read, Ben uttered: "Certain you come again. Come you and eat supper when the wife is not at home."

Gwen quaked as she went to her car, and she sought a person who professed to tell fortunes, and whom she made to say: "A gentleman is in love with you. And he loves you for your brain. He is not your husband. He is more to you than your husband. I hear his silver voice holding spellbound hundreds of people; I see his majestic forehead and his auburn locks and the strands of his silken moustache."

Those words made Gwen very happy, and she deceived herself that they were true. She composed verses and gave them to Ben.

"Not right to Nature is this," said Ben. "The mother is wrong. How many children you have, Messes Enos-Harries?"

"Not one. The husband is weak and he is older much than I."

"The Father has kept His most beautiful gift from you. Pity that is." Tears gushed from Ben's eyes. "If the marriage-maker had brought us together, children we would have jewelled with your eyes and crowned with your hair."

"And your intellect," said Gwen. "You will be the greatest Welshman."

"Whisper will I now. A drag is the wife. Happy you are with the husband."

"Why for you speak like that?"

"And for why we are not married?" Ben took Gwen in his arms and he kissed her and drew her body nigh to him; and in a little while he opened the door sharply and rebuked his wife that she waited thereat.

Daily did Gwen praise and laud Ben to her husband: "There is no one in the world like him," she said. "He will get very far."

"Bring Mistar Lloyd to Windsor for me to know him quite well," said Enoch.

"I will ask him," Gwen replied without faltering.

"Benefit myself I will."

Early every Thursday afternoon Ben arrived at Windsor, and at the coming home from his shop of Enoch, Ben always said: "Messes Enos-Harries has been singing the piano. Like the trilling of God's feathered choir is her music."

Though Ben and Gwen were left at peace they could not satisfy nor crush their lust.

Before three years were over, Ben had obtained great fame. "He ought to be in Parliament and give up preaching entirely," some said; and Enoch and Gwen were partakers of his glory.

Then Gwen told him that she had conceived, whereof Ben counselled her to go into her husband's bed.

"That I have not the stomach to do," the woman

complained.

"As you say, dear heart," said Ben. "Cancer has the wife. Perish soon she must. Smooth our path and lie with your lout."

Presently Gwen bore a child; and Enoch her husband looked at it and said: "Going up is Ben Lloyd. Solid am I as the counter."

Gwen related her fears to Ben, who contrived to make Enoch a member of the London County Council. Enoch rejoiced: summoning the congregation of Thornton Vale to be witnesses of his gift of a Bible cushion to the chapel.

As joy came to him, so grief fell upon his wife. "After all," Ben wrote to her, "you belong to him. You have been joined together in the holiest and sacredest matrimony. Monumental responsibilities have been thrust on me by my people. I did not seek for them, but it is my duty to bear them. Pray that I shall use God's hoe with understanding and wisdom. There is talk of putting me up for Parliament. Others will have a chance of electing a real religious man. I must not be tempted by you again. Well, good-bye, Gwen, may He keep you unspotted from the world. Ships that pass in the night."

Enoch was plagued, and he followed Ben to chapel meetings, eisteddfodau, Cymmrodorion and St David's Day gatherings, always speaking in this fashion: "Cast under is the girl fach you do not visit her. Improved has her singing."

Because Ben was careless of his call, his wrath heated and he said to him: "Growing is the baban."

"How's trade?" Ben remarked. "Do you estimate for Government contracts?"

"Not thought have I."

"Just hinted. A word I can put in."

"Red is the head of the baban."

"Two black heads make red," observed Ben.

"And his name is Benjamin."

"As you speak. Farewell for today. How would you like to put up for a Welsh constituency?"

"Not deserving am I of anything. Happy would I and the wife be to see you in the House."

But Ben's promise was fruitless; and Enoch bewailed: "A serpent flew into my house."

He ordered Gwen to go to Ben.

"Recall to him this and that," he said. "Say that a splendid advert an M.P. would be for the business. Be you dressed like a lady. Take a fur coat on appro from the shop."

Often thereafter he bade his wife to take such a message. But Gwen had overcome her distress and she strew abroad her charms; for no man could now suffice her. So she always departed to one of her lovers and came back with fables on her tongue.

"What can you expect of the Welsh?" cried Enoch in his wrath. "He hasn't paid for the goods he got on tick from the shop. County court him will I. He ate my food. The unrighteous ate the food of the righteous. And he was bad with you. Did I not watch? No good is the assistant that lets the customer go away with not a much obliged."

The portion of the Bible that Enoch read that night was this: "I have decked my bed with coverings of tapestry, with carved works, with fine linen of Egypt... Come, let us take our fill of love until the morning: let us solace ourselves with loves. For the goodman is not at home, he is gone a long journey. He hath ——"

"That's lovely," said Gwen.

"Tapestry from my shop," Enoch expounded. "And Irish linen. And busy was the draper in Kingsend."

Gwen pretended to be asleep.

"He is the father. That will learn him to keep his promise, the wicked man."

Unknown to her husband Gwen stood before Ben; and at the sight of her Ben longed to wanton with her. Gwen stretched out her arms to be clear of him and to speak to him; her speech was stopped with kisses and her breasts swelled out. Again she found pleasure in Ben's strength.

Then she spoke of her husband's hatred.

"Like a Welshman every spit he is," said Ben. "And a black."

But his naughtiness oppressed him for many days and he intrigued; and it came to pass that Enoch was asked to contest a Welsh constituency, and Enoch immediately let fall his anger for Ben.

"Celebrate this we shall with a reception in the Town Hall," he announced. "You, Gwen fach, will wear the chikest Paris model we can find. Ben's kindness is more than I expected. Much that I have I owe to him."

"Even your son," said Gwen.

# LOVE AND HATE

# LOVE AND HATE

BY living frugally — setting aside a portion of his
Civil Service pay and holding all that he got from
two butchers whose trade books he kept in proper
order — Adam Powell became possessed of Cartref
in which he dwelt and which is in Barnes, and two
houses in Thornton East; and one of the houses in
Thornton East he let to his widowed daughter
Olwen, who carried on a dressmaking business. At
the end of his term he retired from his office, his
needs being fulfilled by a pension, and his evening
eased by the ministrations of his elder daughter
Lisbeth.

Soon an inward malady seized him, and in the
belief that he would not be rid of it, he called
Lisbeth and Olwen, to whom both he pronounced
his will.

"The Thornton East property I give you," he
said. "Number seven for Lissi and eight for Olwen
as she is. It will be pleasant to be next door, and
Lissi is not likely to marry at her age which is
advanced. Share and share alike of the furniture,
and what's left sell with the house and haff the proceeds. If you don't fall out in the sharing, you never
will again."

At once Lisbeth and Olwen embraced.

"My sister is my best friend," was the testimony of the elder; "we shan't go astray if we follow the example of the dad and mother," was that of the younger.

"Take two or three excursion trains to Aberporth for the holidays," said Adam, "and get a little gravel for the mother's grave in Beulah. And a cheap artificial wreath. They last better than real ones. It was in Beulah that me and your mother learnt about Jesus."

Together Olwen and Lisbeth pledged that they would attend their father's behests: shunning ill-will and continually petitioning to be translated to the Kingdom of God; "but," Lisbeth laughed false-ly, "you are not going to die. The summer will do wonders for you."

"You are as right as a top really," cried Olwen.

Beholding that his state was the main concern of his children, Adam counted himself blessed; knowing of a surety that the designs of God stand fast against prayer and physic, he said: "I am shiv-ery all over."

A fire was kindled and coals piled upon it that it was scarce to be borne, and three blankets were spread over those which were on his bed, and three earthen bottles which held heated water were put in his bed; and yet the old man got no warmth.

"I'll manage now alone," said Lisbeth on the Saturday morning. "You'll have Jennie and her young gentleman home for Sunday. Should he turn for the worse I'll send for you."

Olwen left, and in the afternoon came Jennie and Charlie from the drapery shop in which they were engaged; and sighing and sobbing she related to them her father's will.

"If I was you, ma," Jennie counselled, "I wouldn't leave him too much alone with Aunt Liz. You never can tell. Funny things may happen."

"I'd trust Aunt Liz anywhere," Olwen declared, loth to have her sister charged with unfaithfulness.

"What do you think, Charlie?" asked Jennie.

The young man stiffened his slender body and inclined his pale face and rubbed his nape, and he proclaimed that there was no discourse of which the meaning was hidden from him and no device with which he was not familiar; and he answered: "I would stick on the spot."

That night Olwen made her customary address to God, and before she came up from her knees or uncovered her eyes, she extolled to God the acts of her father Adam. But slumber kept from her because of that which Jennie had spoken; and diffiding the humour of her heart, she said to herself: "Liz must have a chance of going on with some work." At that she slept; and early in the day she was in Cartref.

"Jennie and Charlie insist you rest," she told Lisbeth. "She can manage quite nicely, and there's Charlie which is a help. So should anyone who is twenty-three."

For a week the daughters waited on their father and contrived they never so wittily to free him from his disorder — Did they not strip and press against him? — they could not deliver him from the wind of dead men's feet. They stitched black cloth into garments and while they stitched they mumbled the doleful hymns of Sion. Two yellow plates were fixed on Adam's coffin — this was in accordance with the man's request — and the engraving on one was in the Welsh tongue, and on the other in the English tongue, and the reason was this; that the angel who lifts the lid — be he of the English or of the Welsh — shall know immediately that the dead is of the people chosen to have the first seats in the Mansion.

The sisters removed from Cartref such things as pleased them; Lisbeth chose more than Olwen, for her house was bare; and in the choosing each gave in to the other, and neither harboured a mean thought.

With her chattels and her sewing machine, Lisbeth entered number seven, which is in Park Villas, and separated from the railway by a wood paling, and from then on the sisters lived by the rare fruits of their joint industry; and never, except on the Sabbath, did they shed their thimbles or the narrow bright scissors which hung from their waists. Some of the poor middle-class folk nearby brought to them their measures of materials, and the more honourable folk who dwelt in the avenues beyond Upper Richmond Road crossed the steep railway bridge with blouses and skirts to be reformed.

"We might be selling Cartref now," said Olwen presently.

"I leave it to you," Lisbeth remarked.

"And I leave it to you. It's as much yours as mine."

"Suppose we consult Charlie?"

"He's a man, and he'll do the best he can."

"Yes, he's very cute is Charlie."

Charlie gave an ear unto Olwen, and he replied: "You been done in. It's disgraceful how she's took everything that were best."

"She had nothing to go on with," said Olwen. "And it will come back. It will be all Jennie's."

"What guarantee have you of that? That's my question. What guarantee?"

Olwen was silent. She was not wishful of disparaging her sister or of squabbling with Charlie.

"Well," said Charlie, "I must have an entirely free hand. Give it an agent if you prefer. They're a lively lot."

He went about over-praising Cartref. "With the sticks and they're not rubbish," he swore, "it's worth five hundred. Three-fifty will buy the lot."

A certain man said to him: "I'll give you two-twenty"; and Charlie replied: "Nothing doing."

Twelve months he was in selling the house, and for the damage which in the meanseason had been done to it by a bomb and by fire and water the sum of money that he received was one hundred and fifty pounds.

Lisbeth had her share, and Olwen had her share, and each applauded Charlie, Lisbeth assuring him: "You'll never regret it"; and this is how Charlie applauded himself: "No one else could have got so much."

"The house and cash will be a nice egg-nest for Jennie," Olwen announced.

"And number seven and mine will make it more," added Lisbeth.

"It's a great comfort that she'll never want a roof over her," said Olwen.

Mindful of their vows to their father, the sisters lived at peace and held their peace in the presence of their prattling neighbours. On Sundays, togged in black gowns on which were ornaments of jet, they worshipped in the Congregational Chapel; and as they stood up in their pew, you saw that Olwen was as the tall trunk of a tree at whose shoulders are the stumps of chopped branches, and that Lisbeth's body was as a billhook. Once they journeyed to Aberporth and they laid a wreath of wax flowers and a thick layer of gravel on their mother's grave. They tore a gap in the wall which divided their little gardens, and their feet, so often did one visit the other, trod a path from backdoor to backdoor.

Nor was their love confused in the joy that each had in Jennie, for whom sacrifices were made and treasures hoarded.

But Jennie was discontented, puling for what she could not have, mourning her lowly fortune, deploring her spinsterhood.

"Charlie and me are getting married Christmas," she said on a day.

"Hadn't you better wait a while," said Olwen. "You're young."

"We talked of that. Charlie is getting on. He's thirty-eight, or will be in January. We'll keep on in the shop and have sleep-out vouchers and come here weekends."

As the manner is, the mother wept.

"You've nothing to worry about," Lisbeth assuaged her sister. "He's steady and respectable. We must see that she does it in style. You look after the other arrangements and I'll see to her clothes."

She walked through wind and rain and sewed by day and night, without heed of the numbness which was creeping into her limbs; and on the floor of a box she put six jugs which had been owned by the Welshwoman who was Adam's grandmother, and over the jugs she arrayed the clothes she had made, and over all she put a piece of paper on which she had written, "To my darling niece from her Aunt Lisbeth."

Jennie examined her aunt's handiwork and was exceedingly wrathful.

"I shan't wear them," she cried. "She might have spoken to me before she started. After all, it's my wedding. Not hers. Pwf! I can buy better jugs in the sixpence-apenny bazaar."

"Aunt Liz will alter them," Olwen began.

"I agree with her," said Charlie. "Aunt Liz should be more considerate seeing what I have done for her. But for me she wouldn't have any money at all."

Charlie and Jennie stirred their rage and gave utterance to the harshest sayings they could devise about Lisbeth; "and I don't care if she's listening outside the door," said Charlie; "and you can tell her it's me speaking," said Jennie.

Throughout Saturday and Sunday Jennie pouted and dealt rudely and uncivilly with her mother; and on Monday, at that hour she was preparing to depart, Olwen relented and gave her twenty pounds, wherefore on the wedding day Lisbeth was astonished.

"Why aren't you wearing my presents ?" she asked.

"That's it," Jennie shouted. "Don't you forget to throw cold water, will you? It wouldn't be you if you did. I don't want to. See? And if you don't like it, lump it."

Olwen calmed her sister, whispering: "She's excited. Don't take notice."

At the quickening of the second dawn after Christmas, Jennie and Charlie arose, and Jennie having hidden her wedding-ring, they two went about their business; and when at noon Olwen proceeded to number seven, she found that Lisbeth had been taken sick of the palsy and was fallen upon the floor. Lisbeth was never well again, and what time she understood all that Olwen had done for her, she melted into tears.

"I should have gone but for you," she averred. "The money's Jennie's, which is the same as I had it and under the mattress, and the house is Jennie's."

"She's fortunate," returned Olwen. "She'll never want for ten shillings a week which it will fetch. You are kind indeed."

"Don't neglect them for me," Lisbeth urged. "I'll be quite happy if you drop in occasionally."

"Are you not my sister?" Olwen cried. "I'm having a bed for you in our front sitting-room. You won't be lonely."

Winter, spring, and summer passed, and the murmurs of Jennie and Charlie against Lisbeth were grown into a horrid clamour.

"Hush, she'll hear you," Olwen always implored. "It won't be for much longer. The doctor says she may go any minute."

"Or last ages," said Charlie.

"Jennie will have the house and the money," Olwen pleaded. "And the money hasn't been touched. Same as you gave it to her. She showed it to me under the mattress. Not everyone have two houses."

"By then you will have bought it over and over again," said Charlie. "Doesn't give Jennie and me much chance of saving, does it?"

"And she can't eat this and can't eat that," Jennie screamed. "She won't, she means."

Weekly was Olwen harassed with new disputes, and she rued that she had said: "I'll have a bed for you in our front sitting-room"; and as it falls out in family quarrels, she sided with her daughter and her daughter's husband.

So the love of the sisters became forced and strained, each speaking and answering with an ill-favoured mouth; it was no longer entire and nothing that was professed united it together.

"I must make my will now," Lisbeth hinted darkly.

"Perhaps Charlie will oblige you," replied Olwen.

"Charlie! You make me smile. Why, he can't keep a wife."

"I thought you had settled all that," Olwen faltered.

"Did you? Anyway, I'll have it in black and white. The minister will do it."

After the minister was gone away, Lisbeth said: "I couldn't very well approach him. He's worried about money for the new vestry. Why didn't you tell me about the new vestry? It was in the magazine."

Olwen mused and from her musings came this: "It'll be a pity to spoil it now. For Jennie's sake."

She got very soft pillows and clean bedclothes for Lisbeth and she placed toothsome dishes before Lisbeth; and it was Lisbeth's way to probe with a fork all the dishes that Olwen had made and to say "It's badly burnt," or "You didn't give much for this," or "Of course you were never taught to cook."

For three years Olwen endured her sister's taunts and the storms of her daughter and her son-in-law; and then Jennie said: "I'm going to have a baby." If she was glad and feared to hear this, how much greater was her joy and how much heavier was her anxiety as Jennie's space grew narrower? She left over going to the aid of Lisbeth, from whom she took away the pillows and for whom she did not provide any more toothsome dishes; she did not go to her aid howsoever frantic the beatings on the wall or fierce the outcry. Never has a sentry kept a closer look-out than Olwen for Jennie. Albeit Jennie died, and as Olwen looked at the hair which was faded from the hue of daffodils into that of tow and at the face the cream of the skin of which was now like clay, she hated Lisbeth with the excess that she had loved her.

"My dear child shall go to Heaven like a Princess," she said; and she sat at her work table to fashion a robe of fine cambric and lace for her dead.

Disturbed by the noise of the machine, Lisbeth wailed: "You let me starve but won't let me sleep. Why doesn't any one help me? I'll get the fever. What have I done?"

Olwen moved to the doorway of the room, her

body filling the frame thereof, her scissors hanging at her side.

"You are wrong, sister, to starve me," Lisbeth said. "To starve me. I cannot walk you know. You must not blame me if I change my mind about my money. It was wrong of you."

Olwen did not answer.

"Dear me," Lisbeth cried, "supposing our father in Heaven knew how you treat me. Indeed the vestry shall have my bit. I might be a pig in a pigstye. I'll get the fever. Supposing our father is looking through the window of Heaven at your cruelty to me."

Olwen muttered the burden of her care: "'The wife would pull through if she had plenty of attention. How could she with her about? The two of you killed her. You did. I warned you to give up everything and see to her. But you neglected her.' That's what Charlie will say. Hoo-hoo. 'It's unheard of for a woman to die before childbirth. Serves you right if I have an inquest.'..."

"For shame to keep from me now," said Lisbeth in a voice that was higher than the continued muttering of Olwen. "Have you no regard for the living? The dead is dead. And you made too much of Jennie. You spoiled her...."

On a sudden Olwen ceased, and she strode up to the bed and thrust her scissors into Lisbeth's breast.

TREASURE AND TROUBLE

# TREASURE AND TROUBLE

ON a day in a dry summer Sheremiah's wife Catrin drove her cows to drink at the pistil which is in the field of a certain man. Hearing of that which she had done, the man commanded his son: "Awful is the frog to open my gate. Put you the dog and bitch on her. Teach her will I."

It was so; and Sheremiah complained: "Why for is my spring barren? In every field should water be."

"Say, little husband, what is in your think?" asked Catrin.

"Stupid is your head," Sheremiah answered, "not to know what I throw out. Going am I to search for a wet farm fach."

Sheremiah journeyed several ways, and always he journeyed in secret; and he could not find what he wanted. Tailor Club Foot came to sit on his table to sew together garments for him and his two sons. The tailor said: "Farm very pretty is Rhydwen. Farm splendid is the farm fach."

"And speak like that you do, Club Foot," said Sheremiah.

"Iss-iss," the tailor mumbled.

"Not wanting an old farm do I," Sheremiah cried. "But speak to goodness where the place is. Near you are, calf bach, about affairs."

The tailor answered that Rhydwen is in the hollow of the hill which arises from Capel Sion to the moor.

In the morning Sheremiah rode forth on his colt, and he said to Shan Rhydwen: "Boy of a pigger am I, whatever."

"Dirt-dirt, man," Shan cried; "no fat pigs have I, look you."

"Mournful that is. Mouthings have I heard about grand pigs Tyhen. No odds, wench. Farewell for this minute, female Tyhen."

"Pigger from where you are?" Shan asked.

"From Pencader the horse has carried me. Carry a preacher he did the last Monday."

"Weary you are, stranger. Give hay to your horse, and rest you and take you a little cup of tea."

"Happy am I to do that. Thirsty is the backhead of my neck."

Sheremiah praised the Big Man for tea, bread, butter, and cheese, and while he ate and drank he put artful questions to Shan. In the evening he said to Catrin: "Quite tidy is Rhydwen. Is she not one hundred acres? And if there is not water in every field, is there not in four?"

He hastened to the owner of Rhydwen and made this utterance: "Farmer very ordinary is your sister Shan. Shamed was I to examine your land."

"I shouldn't be surprised," answered the owner. "Speak hard must I to the trollop."

"Not handy are women," said Sheremiah. "Sell him to me the poor-place. Three-fourths of the cost I give in yellow money and one-fourth by-and-by in three years."

Having taken over Rhydwen, Sheremiah in due season sold much of his corn and hay, some of his cattle, and many such moveable things as were in his house or employed in tillage; and he and Catrin came to abide in Rhydwen; and they arrived with horses in carts, cows, a bull and oxen, and their sons, Aben and Dan. As they passed Capel Sion, people who were gathered at the roadside to judge them remarked how that Aben was blind in his left eye and that Dan's shoulders were as high as his ears.

At the finish of a round of time Sheremiah hired out his sons and all that they earned he took away from them; and he and Catrin toiled to recover Rhydwen from its slovenry. After he had paid all that he owed for the place, and after Catrin had died of dropsy, he called his sons home.

Thereon he thrived. He was over all on the floor of Sion, even those in the Big Seat. Men in debt and many widow-women sought him to free them, and in freeing them he made compacts to his advantage. Thus he came to have more cattle than Rhydwen could hold, and he bought Penlan, the farm of eighty acres which goes up from Rhydwen to the edge of the moor, and beyond.

In quiet seasons he and Aben and Dan dug ditches on the land of Rhydwen; "so that," he said, "my creatures shall not perish of thirst."

Of a sudden a sickness struck him, and in the hush which is sometimes before death, he summoned to him his sons. "Off away am I to the Palace," he said.

"Large will be the shout of joy among the

angels," Aben told him.

"And much weeping there will be in Sion," said Dan. "Speak you a little verse for a funeral preach."

"Cease you your babblings, now, indeed," Sheremiah demanded. "Born first you were, Aben, and you get Rhydwen. And you, Dan, Penlan."

"Father bach," Aben cried, " not right that you leave more to me than Dan."

"Crow you do like a cuckoo," Dan admonished his brother. "Wise you are, father. Big already is your giving to me."

Aben looked at the window and he beheld a corpse candle moving outward through the way of the gate. "Religious you lived, father Sheremiah, and religious you put on a White Shirt." Then Aben spoke of the sight he had seen.

The old man opened his lips, counselling: "Hish, hish, boys. Break you trenches in Penlan, Dan. Poor bad are farms without water. More than everything is water." He died, and his sons washed him and clothed him in a White Shirt of the dead, and clipped off his long beard, which ceasing to grow, shall not entwine his legs and feet and his arms and hands on the Day of Rising; and they bowed their heads in Sion for the full year.

Dan and Aben lived in harmony. They were not as brothers, but as strangers; neighbourly and at peace. They married wives, by whom they had children, and they sat in the Big Seat in Sion. They mowed their hay and reaped their corn at separate periods, so that one could help the other; if one needed the loan of anything he would borrow it from his brother; if one's heifer strayed into the pasture of the other, the other would say: "The Big Man will make the old grass grow." On the Sabbath they and their children walked as in procession to Sion.

In accordance with his father's word, Dan dug ditches in Penlan; and against the barnyard — which is at the forehead of his house — water sprang up, and he caused it to run over his water-wheel into his pond.

Now there fell upon this part of Cardiganshire a season of exceeding drought. The face of the earth was as the face of a cancerous man. There was no water in any of the ditches of Rhydwen and none in those of Penlan. But the spring which Dan had found continued to yield, and from it Aben's wife took away water in pitchers and buckets; and to the pond Aben brought his animals.

One day Aben spoke to Dan in this wise: "Serious sure, an old bother is this."

"Iss-iss," replied Dan. "Good is the Big Man to allow us water bach."

"How speech you if I said: 'Unfasten your pond and let him flow into my ditches'?"

"The land will suck him before he goes far," Dan answered.

Aben departed; and he considered: "Did not Penlan belong to Sheremiah? Travel under would the water and hap spout up in my close. Nice that would be. Nasty is the behaviour of Dan and there's sly is the iob."

To Dan he said: "Open your pond, man, and let the water come into the ditches which father Sheremiah broke."

Dan would not do as Aben desired, wherefore Aben informed against him in Sion, crying: "Little Big Man, know you not what a Turk is the fox? One eye bach I have, but you have two, and can see all his wickedness. Make you him pay the cost." He raised his voice so high that the congregation could not discern the meaning thereof, and it shouted as one person: "Wo, now, boy Sheremiah! What is the matter, say you? "

The anger which Aben nourished against Dan waxed hot. Rain came, and it did not abate, and the man plotted mischief to his brother's damage. In heavy darkness he cut the halters which held Dan's cows and horses to their stalls and drove the animals into the road. He also poisoned pond Penlan, and a sheep died before it could be killed and eaten.

Dan wept very sore. "Take you the old water," he said. "Fat is my sorrow."

"Not religious you are," Aben censured him. "All the water is mine."

"Useful he is to me," Dan replied. "Like would I that he turns my wheel as he goes to you."

"Clap your mouth," answered Aben. "Not as much as will go through the leg of a smoking pipe shall you have."

In Sion Aben told the Big Man of all the benefits which he had conferred upon Dan.

Men and women encouraged his fury; some said this: "An old paddy is Dan to rob your water. Ach y fi"; and some said this: "A dirty ass is the mule." His fierce wrath was not allayed albeit Dan turned the course of the water away from his pond, and on his knees and at his labour asked God that peace might come.

"Bury the water," Aben ordered, "and fill in the ditch, Satan."

"That will I do speedily," Dan answered in his timidity. "Do you give me an hour fach, for is not the sowing at hand?" Aben would not hearken unto his brother. He deliberated with a lawyer, and Dan was made to dig a ditch straightway from the spring to the close of Rhydwen, and he put pipes in the bottom of the ditch, and these pipes he covered with gravel and earth.

So as Dan did not sow, he had nothing to reap; and people mocked him in this fashion: "Come we will and gather in your harvest, Dan bach." He held his tongue, because he had nothing to say. His affliction pressed upon him so heavily that he would not be consoled and he hanged himself on a tree; and his body was taken down at the time of the morning stars.

A man ran to Rhydwen and related to Aben the manner of Dan's death. Aben went into a field and sat as one astonished until the light of day paled. Then he arose, shook himself, and set to number the ears of wheat which were in his field.

# SAINT DAVID AND THE PROPHETS

# SAINT DAVID AND THE PROPHETS

GOD grants prayers gladly. In the moment that Death was aiming at him a missile of down, Hughes-Jones prayed: "Bad I've been. Don't let me fall into the Fiery Pool. Give me a brief while and a grand one I'll be for the religion." A shaft of fire came out of the mouth of the Lord and the shaft stood in the way of the missile, consuming it utterly; "so," said the Lord, "are his offences forgotten."

"Is it a light thing," asked Paul, "to defy the Law?"

"God is merciful," said Moses.

"Is the Kingdom for such as pray conveniently?"

"This," Moses reproved Paul, "is written in a book: 'The Lord shall judge His people.'"

Yet Paul continued to dispute, the Prophets gathering near him for entertainment; and the company did not break up until God, as is the custom in Heaven when salvation is wrought, proclaimed a period of rejoicing.

Wherefore Heaven's windows, the number of which is more than that of blades of grass in the biggest hayfield, were lit as with a flame; and Heman and his youths touched their instruments with fingers and hammers and the singing angels lifted their voices in song; and angels in the likeness of young girls brewed tea in urns and angels in the likeness of old women baked pleasant breads in the heavenly ovens. Out of Hell there arose two mountains, which established themselves one over the other on the floor of Heaven, and the height of the mountains was the depth of Hell; and you could not see the sides of the mountains for the vast multitude of sinners thereon, and you could not see the sinners for the live coals to which they were held, and you could not see the burning coals for the radiance of the pulpit which was set on the furthermost peak of the mountain, and you could not see the pulpit — from toe to head it was of pure gold — for the shining countenance of Isaiah; and as Isaiah preached, blood issued out of the ends of his fingers from the violence with which he smote his Bible, and his single voice was louder than the lamentations of the damned.

As the Lord had enjoined, the inhabitants of Heaven rejoiced: eating and drinking, weeping and crying hosanna.

But Paul would not joy over that which the Lord had done, and soon he sought Him, and finding Him said: "A certain Roman noble laboured his horses to their death in a chariot race before Cæsar: was he worthy of Cæsar's reward?"

"The noble is on the mountainside," God answered, "and his horses are in my chariots."

"One bears witness to his own iniquity, and you bid us feast and you say 'He shall have remembrance of me.'"

"Is there room in Heaven for a false witness?" asked God.

Again did Paul seek God. "My Lord," he entreated, "what manner of man is this that confesses his faults?"

"You will provoke my wrath," said God. "Go and be merry."

Paul's face being well turned, God moved backward into the Record Office, and of the Clerk of the Records He demanded: "Who is he that prayed unto me?"

"William Hughes-Jones," replied the Clerk.

"Has the Forgiving Angel blotted out his sins?"

"For that I have fixed a long space of time"; and the Clerk showed God eleven heavy books, on the outside of each of which was written: "William Hughes-Jones, One and All Drapery Store, Hammersmith. His sins"; and God examined the books and was pleased, and He cried: "Rejoice fourfold"; and if Isaiah's roar was higher than the wailings of the perished it was now more awful than the roar of a hundred bullocks in a slaughterhouse, and if Isaiah's countenance shone more than anything in Heaven, it was now like the eye of the sun.

"Of what nation is he?" the Lord inquired of the Clerk.

"The Welsh; the Welsh Nonconformists."

"Put before me their good deeds."

"There is none. William Hughes-Jones is the first of them that has prayed. Are not the builders making a chamber for the accounts of their disobedience?"

Immediately God thundered: the earth trembled and the stars shivered and fled from their courses and struck against one another; and God stood on the brim of the universe and stretched out a hand and a portion of a star fell into it, and that is the portion which He hurled into the garden of Hughes-Jones's house. On a sudden the revels ceased: the bread of the feast was stone and the tea water, and the songs of the angels were hushed, and the strings of the harps and viols were withered, and the hammers were dough, and the mountains sank into Hell, and behold Satan in the pulpit which was an iron cage.

The Prophets hurried into the Judgment Hall with questions, and lo God was in a cloud, and He spoke out of the cloud.

"I am angry," He said, "that Welsh Nonconformists have not heard my name. Who are the Welsh Nonconformists?" The Prophets were silent, and God mourned: "My Word is the earth and I peopled the earth with my spittle; and I appointed my Prophets to watch over my people, and the watchers slept and my children strayed."

Thus too said the Lord: "That hour I devour my children who have forsaken me, that hour I shall devour my Prophets."

"May be there is one righteous among us?" said Moses.

"You have all erred."

"May be there is one righteous among the Nonconformists," said Moses; "will the just God destroy him?"

"The one righteous is humbled, and I have warned him to keep my commandments."

"The sown seed brought forth a prayer," Moses

pleaded; "will not the just God wait for the harvest?"

"My Lord is just," Paul announced. "They who gather wickedness shall not escape the judgment, nor shall the blind instructor be held blameless."

Moreover Paul said: "The Welsh Nonconformists have been informed of you as is proved by the man who confessed his transgressions. It is a good thing for me that I am not of the Prophets."

"I'll be your comfort, Paul," the Prophets murmured, "that you have done this to our hurt." Abasing themselves, they tore their mantles and howled; and God, piteous of their howlings, was constrained to say: "Bring me the prayers of these people and I will forget your remissness."

The Prophets ran hither and thither, wailing: "Woe. Woe. Woe."

Sore that they behaved with such scant respect, Paul herded them into the Council Room. "Is it seemly," he rebuked them, "that the Prophets of God act like madmen?"

"Our lot is awful," said they.

"The lot of the backslider is justifiably awful," was Paul's reminder. "You have prophesied too diligently of your own glory."

"You are learned in the Law, Paul," said Moses. "Make us waywise."

"Send abroad a messenger to preach damnation to sinners," answered Paul. "For Heaven," added he, "is the knowledge of Hell."

So it came to pass. From the hem of Heaven's Highway an angel flew into Wales; and the angel, having judged by his sight and his hearing, returned to the Council Room and testified to the godliness of the Welsh Nonconformists. "As difficult for me," he vowed, "to write the feathers of my wings as the sum of their daily prayers."

"None has reached the Record Office," said Paul.

"They are always engaged in this bright business," the angel declared, "and praising the Lord. And the number of the people is many and Heaven will need be enlarged for their coming."

"Of a surety they pray?" asked Paul.

"Of a surety. And as they pray they quake terribly."

"The Romans prayed hardly," said Paul. "But they prayed to other gods."

"Wherever you stand on their land," asserted the angel, "you see a temple."

"I exceedingly fear," Paul remarked, "that another Lord has dominion over them."

The Prophets were alarmed, and they sent a company of angels over the earth and a company under the earth; and the angels came back; one company said: "We searched the swampy marges and saw neither a god nor a heaven nor any prayer," and the other company said: "We probed the lofty emptiness and we did not touch a god or a heaven or any prayer."

Paul was distressed and he reported his misgivings to God, and God upbraided the Prophets for their sloth. "Is there no one who can do this for me?" He cried. "Are all the cunning men in Hell? Shall I make all Heaven drink the dregs of my fury? Burnish your rusted armour. Depart into Hell and cry out: 'Is there one here who knows the Welsh Nonconformists?' Choose the most crafty and release him and lead him here."

Lots were cast and it fell to Moses to descend into Hell; and he stood at the well, the water of which is harder than crystal, and he cried out; and of the many that professed he chose Saint David, whom he brought up to God.

"Visit your people," said God to the Saint, "and bring me their prayers."

"Why should I be called?"

"It is my will. My Prophets have failed me, and if it is not done they shall be destroyed."

David laughed. "From Hell comes a saviour of the Prophets. In the middle of my discourse at the Judgment Seat the Prophets stooped upon me. 'To Hell with him,' they screamed."

"Perform faithfully," said the Lord, "and you shall remain in Paradise."

"My Lord is gracious! I was a Prophet and the living believe that I am with the saints. I will retire."

"Perform faithfully and you shall be of my Prophets."

Then God took away David's body and nailed it upon a wall, and He put wings on the shoulders of his soul; and David darted through a cloud and landed on earth, and having looked at the filthiness of the Nonconformists in Wales he withdrew to London. But however actively he tried he could not find a man of God nor the destination of the fearful prayers of Welsh preachers, grocers, drapers, milkmen, lawyers, and politicians.

Loth to go to Hell and put to a nonplus, David

built a nest in a tree in Richmond Park, and he
paused therein to consider which way to proceed.
One day he was disturbed by the singing and
preaching of a Welsh soldier who had taken shelter
from rain under the tree. David came down from his
nest, and when the mouth of the man was most
open, he plunged into the fellow's body.
Henceforward in whatsoever place the soldier was
there also was David; and the soldier carried him to
a clothier's shop in Putney, the sign of the shop
being written in this fashion:

J, Parker Lewis.
The Little (Gents. Mercer) Wonder.

Crossing the threshold, the soldier shouted:
"How you are?"

The clothier, whose skin was as hide which has
been scorched in a tanner's yard, bent over the
counter. "Man bach," he exclaimed, "glad am I to
see you. Pray will I now that you are all Zer
Garnett." His thanksgiving finished, he said:
"Wanting a suit you do."

"Yes, and no," replied the soldier. "Cheap she
must be if yes."

"You need one for certain. Shabby you are."

"This is a friendly call. To a low-class shop
must a poor tommy go.

"Do you then not be cheated by an English
swindler." The clothier raised his thin voice: "Kate,
here's a strange boy."

A pretty young woman, in spite of her snaggled
teeth, frisked into the room like a wanton lamb. Her

brown hair was drawn carelessly over her head, and her flesh was packed but loosely. "Serious me," she cried, "Llew Eevans! Llew bach, how you are? Very big has the army made you and strong."

"Not changed you are."

"No. The last time you came was to see the rabbit."

"Dear me, yes. Have you still got her?"

"She's in the belly long ago," said the clothier.

"I have another in her stead," said Kate. "A splendid one. Would you like to fondle her?"

"Why, yez," answered the soldier.

"Drat the old animal," cried the clothier. "Too much care you give her, Kate. Seven looks has the deacon from Capel King's Cross had of her and he hasn't bought her yet."

As he spoke the clothier heaped garments on the counter.

"Put out your arms," he ordered Kate, "and take the suits to a room for Llew to try on."

Kate obeyed, and Llew hymning "Moriah" took her round the waist and embraced her, and the woman, hungering for love gladly gave herself up. Soon attired in a black frock coat, a black waistcoat, and black trousers, Llew stepped into the shop.

"A champion is the rabbit," he said; "and very tame."

"If meat doesn't come down," said the clothier, "in the belly she'll be as well."

"Let me know before you slay her. Perhaps I buy her. I will study her again."

The clothier gazed upon Llew. "Tidy fit," he said.

91

"A bargain you give me."

"Why for you talk like that?" the clothier protested. "No profit can I make on a Cymro. As per invoice is the cost. And a latest style bowler hat I throw in."

Peering through Llew's body, Saint David saw that the dealer dealt treacherously, and that the money which he got for the garments was two pounds over that which was proper.

Llew walked away whistling. "A simple fellow is the black," he said to himself. "Three soverens was bad."

On the evening of the next day — that day being the Sabbath — the soldier worshipped in Capel Kingsend; and betwixt the sermon and the benediction, the preacher delivered this speech: "Very happy am I to see so many warriors here once more. We sacrificed for them quite a lot, and if they have any Christianity left in them they will not forget what Capel Kingsend has done and will repay same with interest. Happier still we are to welcome Mister Hughes-Jones to the Big Seat. In the valley of the shadow has Mister Hughes-Jones been. Earnestly we prayed for our dear religious leader. Tomorrow at seven we shall hold a prayer meeting for his cure. At seven at night. Will everybody remember? On Monday — tomorrow — at seven at night a prayer meeting for Mister Hughes-Jones will be held in Capel Kingsend. The duty of everyone is to attend. Will you please say something now, zer?"

Hughes-Jones rose from the armchair which is under the pulpit, and thrust out his bristled chin and rested his palms on the communion table; and he said not one word.

"Mister Hughes-Jones," the preacher urged.

"I am too full of grace," said Hughes-Jones; he spoke quickly, as one who is on the verge of tears, and his big nostrils widened and narrowed as those of one who is short of breath.

"The congregation, zer, expects ——"

"Well-well, I've had a glimpse of the better land and with a clear conscience I could go there, only the Great Father has more for me to do here. A miracle happened to me. In the thick of my sickness a meetority dropped outside the bedroom. The mistress fainted slap bang. 'If this is my summons,' I said, 'I am ready.' A narrow squeak that was. I will now sit and pray for you one and all."

In the morning Llew went to the One and All and in English — that is the tongue of the high Welsh — did he address Hughes-Jones.

"I've come to start, zer," he said.

"Why wassn't you in the chapel yezterday?"

"I wass there, zer."

"Ho-ho. For me there are two people in the chapel — me and Him."

"Yez, indeed. Shall I gommence now?"

"Gommence what?"

"My crib what I leave to join up."

"Things have changed. There has been a war on, mister. They are all smart young ladies here now. And it is not right to sack them and shove them on the streets."

"But ——"

"Don't answer back, or I'll have you chucked

from the premizes and locked up. Much gratitude you show for all I did for the soders."

"Beg pardon, zer."

"We too did our bits at home. Slaved like horses. Me and the two sons. And they had to do work of national importance. Disgraceful I call it in a free country."

"I would be much obliged, zer, if you would take me on."

"You left on your own accord, didn't you? I never take back a hand that leave on their own. Why don't you be patriotic and rejoin and finish up the Huns?"

Bowed down, the soldier made himself drunk, and the drink enlivened his dismettled heart; and in the evening he stole into the loft which is above the Big Seat of Capel Kingsend, purposing to disturb the praying men with loud curses.

But Llew slept, and while he slept the words of the praying men came through the ceiling like the pieces of a child's jigsaw puzzle; some floated sluggishly and fell upon the wall and the roof, and some because of their little strength did not reach above the floor; and none went through the roof. Saint David closed his hands on many, and there was no soundness in them, and they became as though they were nothing. He formed a bag of the soldier's handkerchief, and he filled it with the words, but as he drew to the edges they crumbled into less than dust.

He pondered; and he made a sack out of cobwebs, and when the sack could not contain any more words, he wove a lid of cobwebs over the mouth of it. Jealous that no mishap should befall his treasure, he mounted a low, slow-moving cloud, and folding his wings rode up to the Gate of the Highway.

# JOSEPH'S HOUSE

# JOSEPH'S HOUSE

A WOMAN named Madlen, who lived in Penlan —
the crumbling mud walls of which are in a nook of
the narrow lane that rises from the valley of Bern —
was concerned about the future state of her son
Joseph. Men who judged themselves worthy to
counsel her gave her such counsels as these:
"Blower bellows for the smith," "Cobblar clox,"
"Booboo for crows."

Madlen flattered her counsellors, albeit none
spoke that which was pleasing unto her.

"Cobblar clox, ach y fy," she cried to herself.
"Wan is the lad bach with decline. And unbecoming
to his Nuncle Essec that he follows low tasks."

Moreover, people, look you at John Lewis.
Study his marble gravestone in the burial ground of
Capel Sion: "His name is John Newton-Lewis;
Paris House, London, his address. From his big
shop in Putney, Home they brought him by railway." Genteel are shops for boys who are con-
sumptive. Always dry are their coats and feet, and
they have white cuffs on their wrists and chains on
their waistcoats. Not blight nor disease nor frost can
ruin their sellings. And every minute their fingers
grabble in the purses of nobles.

So Madlen thought, and having acted in accordance with her design, she took her son to the other

side of Avon Bern, that is to Capel Mount Moriah, over which Essec her husband's brother lorded; and him she addressed decorously, as one does address a ruler of the capel.

"Your help I seek," she said.

"Poor is the reward of the Big Preacher's son in this part," Essec announced. "A lot of atheists they are."

"Not pleading I have not the rent am I," said Madlen. "How if I prentice Joseph to a shop draper. Has he any odds? "

"Proper that you seek," replied Essec. "Seekers we all are. Sit you. No room there is for Joseph now I am selling Penlan."

"Like that is the plan of your head?" Madlen murmured, concealing her dread.

"Seven of pounds of rent is small. Sell at eighty I must."

"Wait for Joseph to prosper. Buy then he will. Buy for your mam you will, Joseph?"

"Sorry I cannot change my think," Essec declared.

"Hard is my lot; no male have I to ease my burden."

"A weighty responsibility my brother put on me," said Essec. "'Dying with old decline I am,' the brother mouthed. 'Fruitful is the soil. Watch Madlen keeps her fruitful.' But I am generous. Eight shall be the rent. Are you not the wife of my flesh?"

After she had wiped away her tears, "Be kind," said Madlen, "and wisdom it to Joseph."

"The last evening in the Seiet I commanded the

congregation to give the Big Man's photograph a larger hire," said Essec. "A few of my proverbs I will now spout." He spat his spittle and bundling his beard blew the residue of his nose therein; and he chanted: "Remember Essec Pugh, whose right foot is tied into a club knot. Here's the club to kick sinners as my perished brother tried to kick the Bad Satan from the inside of his female Madlen with the club of his baston. Some preachers search over the Word. Some preachers search in the Word. But search under the Word does preacher Capel Moriah. What's the light I find? A stutterer was Moses. As the middle of a butter cask were the knees of Paul. A splotch like a red cabbage leaf was on the cheek of Solomon. By the signs shall the saints be known. 'Preacher Club Foot, come forward to tell about Moriah,' the Big Man will say. Mean scamps, remember Essec Pugh, for I shall remember you the Day of Rising."

It came to be that on a morning in the last month of his thirteenth year Joseph was bidden to stand at the side of the cow which Madlen was milking and to give an ear to these commandments: "The serpent is in the bottom of the glass. The hand on the tavern window is the hand of Satan. On the Sabbath eve get one penny for two ha'pennies for the plate collection. Put money in the handkerchief corner. Say to persons you are a nephew of Respected Essec Pugh and you will have credit. Pick the white sixpence from the floor and give her to the mishtir; she will have fallen from his pocket trowis."

Then Joseph turned, and carrying his yellow tin

box, he climbed into the craggy moorland path which takes you to the tramping road. By the pump of Tavarn Ffos he rested until Shim Carrier came thereby; and while Shim's horse drank of barley water, Joseph stepped into the waggon; and at the end of the passage Shim showed him the business of getting a ticket and that of going into and coming down from a railway carriage.

In that manner did Joseph go to the drapery shop of Rees Jones in Carmarthen; and at the beginning he was instructed in the keeping and the selling of such wares as reels of cotton, needles, pins, bootlaces, mending wool, buttons, and such like — all those things which together are known as haberdashery. He marked how this and that were done, and in what sort to fashion his visage and frame his phrases to this or that woman. His oncoming was rapid. He could measure, cut, and wrap in a parcel twelve yards of brown or white calico quicker than anyone in the shop, and he understood by rote the folds of linen tablecloths and bedsheets; and in the town this was said of him: "Shopmen quite ordinary can sell what a customer wants; Pugh Rees Jones can sell what nobody wants."

The first year passed happily, and the second year; and in the third Joseph was stirred to go forward.

"What use to stop here all the life?" he asked himself. "Better to go off."

He put his belongings in his box and went to Swansea.

"Very busy emporium I am in," were the words

he sent to Madlen. "And the wage is twenty pounds."

Madlen rejoiced at her labour and sang: "Ten acres of land, and a cowhouse with three stalls and a stall for the new calf, and a pigstye, and a house for my bones and a barn for my hay and straw, and a loft for my hens: why should men pray for more?" She ambled to Moriah, diverting passers-by with boastful tales of Joseph, and loosened her imaginings to the Respected.

"Pounds without number he is earning," she cried. "Rich he'll be. Swells are youths shop."

"Gifts from the tip of my tongue fell on him," said Essec. "Religious were my gifts."

"Iss, indeed, the brother of the male husband."

"Now you can afford nine of pounds for the place. Rich he is and richer he will be. Pounds without number he has."

Madlen made a record of Essec's scheme for Joseph; and she said also: "Proud I'll be to shout that my son bach bought Penlan."

"Setting aside money am I," Joseph speedily answered.

Again ambition aroused him. "Footling is he that is content with Zwanssee. Next half-holiday skurshon I'll crib in Cardiff."

Joseph gained his desire, and the chronicle of his doings he sent to his mother. "Twenty-five, living-in, and spiffs on remnants are the wages," he said. "In the flannelette department I am and I have not been fined once. Lot of English I hear, and we call ladies madam that the wedded nor the unwedded are insulted. Boys harmless are the eight that sleep by me. Examine Nuncle of the price of Penlan."

"I will wag my tongue craftily and slowly," Madlen vowed as she crossed her brother-in-law's threshold.

"In Shire Pembroke land is cheap," she said darkly.

"Look you for a farm there," said Essec. "Pelted with offers am I for Penlan. Ninety I shall have. Poverty makes me sell very soon."

"As he says."

"Pretty tight is Joseph not to buy her. No care has he for his mam."

"Stiffish are affairs with him, poor dab."

Madlen reported to Joseph that which Essec had said, and she added: "Awful to leave the land of your father. And auction the cows. Even the red cow that is a champion for milk. Where shall I go? The House of the Poor. Horrid that your mam must go to the House of the Poor."

Joseph sat on his bed, writing: "Taken ten pounds from the post I have which leaves three shillings. Give Nuncle the ten as earnest of my intention."

Nine years after that day on which he had gone to Carmarthen Joseph said in his heart: "London shops for experience"; and he caused a frock coat to be sewn together, and he bought a silk hat and an umbrella, and at the spring cribbing he walked into a shop in the West End of London, asking: "Can I see the engager, pleaze?" The engager came to him and Joseph spoke out: "I have all-round experience. Flannelettes three years in Niclass, Cardiff, and left on my own accord. Kept the coloured dresses in Tomos, Zwanssee. And served through. Apprentized in Reez Jones Carmarthen for three years. Refs egzellent. Good ztok-keeper and appearance."

"Start at nine o'clock Monday morning," the engager replied. "Thirty pounds a year and spiffs; to live in. You'll be in the laces."

"Fashionable this shop is," Joseph wrote to Madlen, "and I have to be smart and wear a coat like the preachers, and mustn't take more than three zwap lines per day or you have the sack. Two white shirts per week; and the dresses of the showroom young ladies are a treat. Five pounds enclosed for Nuncle."

"Believe your mam," Madlen answered: "don't throw gravel at the windows of the old English unless they have the fortunes."

In his zeal for his mother's welfare Joseph was heedless of himself, eating little of the poor food that was served him, clothing his body niggardly, and seldom frequenting public bath houses; his mind spanned his purpose, choosing the fields he would join to Penlan, counting the number of cattle that would graze on the land, planning the slate-tiled house which he would set up.

"Twenty pounds more must I have," he moaned, "for the blaguard Nuncle."

Every day thereafter he stole a little money from his employers and every night he made peace with God: "Only twenty-five is the wage, and spiffs don't count because of the fines. Don't you let me be found out, Big Man bach. Will you strike mam into her grave? And disgrace Respected Essec Pugh Capel Moriah?"

He did not abate his energies howsoever hard his disease was wasting and destroying him. The men who lodged in his bedroom grew angry with him. "How can we sleep with your dam coughing?" they cried. "Why don't you invest in a second-hand coffin?"

Feared that the women whom he served would complain that the poison of his sickness was tainting them and that he would be sent away, Joseph increased his pilferings; where he had stolen a shilling he now stole two shillings; and when he got five pounds above the sum he needed, he heaved a deep sigh and said: "Thank you for your favour, God bach. I will now go home to heal myself."

Madlen took the money to Essec, coming back heavy with grief.

"Hoo-hoo," she whined, "the ninety has bought only the land. Selling the houses is Essec."

"Wrong there is," said Joseph. "Probe deeply we must."

From their puzzlings Madlen said: "What will you do?"

"Go and charge swindler Moriah."

"Meddle not with him. Strong he is with the Lord."

"Teach him will I to pocket my honest wealth."

Because of his weakness, Joseph did not go to Moriah; to-day he said: "I will tomorrow," and to-morrow he said: "Certain enough I'll go tomor-row."

In the twilight of an afternoon he and Madlen

sat down, gazing about, and speaking scantily; and the same thought was with each of them, and this was the thought: "A tearful prayer will remove the Big Man from His judgment but nothing will remove Essec from his purpose."

"Mam fach," said Joseph "how will things be with you? "

"Sorrow not, soul nice," Madlen entreated her son. "Couple of weeks very short have I to live."

"As an hour is my space. Who will stand up for you?"

"Hish, now. Hish-hish, my little heart."

Madlen sighed; and at the door she made a great clatter, and the sound of the clatter was less than the sound of her wailing.

"Mam! Mam!" Joseph shouted. "Don't you scream. Hap you will soften Nuncle's heart if you say to him that my funeral is close."

Madlen put a mourning gown over her petticoats and a mourning bodice over her shawls, and she tarried in a field as long as it would take her to have travelled to Moriah; and in the heat of the sun she returned, laughing.

"Mistake, mistake," she cried. "The houses are ours. No understanding was in me. Cross was your Nuncle. 'Terrible if Joseph is bad with me,' he said. Man religious and tidy is Essec." Then she prayed that Joseph would die before her fault was found out.

Joseph did not know what to do for his joy. "Well-well, there's better I am already," he said. He walked over the land and coveted the land of his neighbours. "Dwell here for ever I shall," he cried to Madlen. "A grand house I'll build — almost as grand as the houses of preachers."

In the fifth night he died, and before she began to weep, Madlen lifted her voice: "There's silly, dear people, to covet houses! Only a smallish bit of house we want."

LIKE BROTHERS

# LIKE BROTHERS

SILAS BOWEN hated his brother John, but when he heard of John's sickness, he reasoned: "Blackish has been his dealings. And trickish. Sly also. Odd will affairs seem if I don't go to him at once." At the proper hour he closed the door of his shop. Then he washed his face, and put beeswax on the dwindling points of his moustache, and he came out of Barnes into Thornton East; into High Road, where is his brother's shop.

"That is you," said John to him.

"How was you, man?" Silas asked. "Talk the name of the old malady."

"Say what you have to say in English," John answered in a little voice. "It is easier and classier."

That which was spoken was rendered into English; and John replied: "I am pleazed to see you. Take the bowler off your head and don't put her on the harimonium. The zweat will mark the wood."

"The love of brothers push me here," said Silas. "It is past understanding. As boyss we learn the same pray-yer. And we talked the same temperance dialogue in Capel Zion. I was always the temperance one. And quite a champion reziter. The way is round and about, boy bach, from Zion to the grave."

"Don't speak like that," pleaded John. "I caught a cold going to the City to get ztok. I will be healthy

111

by the beginning of the week."

"Be it so. Yet I am full of your trouble. Sick you are and how's trade?"

"Very brisk. I am opening a shop in Richmond again," John said.

"You're learning me something. Don't you think too much of that shop; Death is near, and set your mind on the crossing."

John's lame daughter Ann halted into the room, and stepped up to the bed.

"Stand by the door for one minit, Silas," John cried. "I am having my chat confidential."

From a book Ann recited the business of that day; naming each article that had been sold, and the cost and the profit thereof.

"How's that with last year?" her father commanded.

"Two-fifteen below."

"Fool!" John whispered. "You are a cow, with your gamey leg. You're ruining the place."

Ann closed the book and put her fountain pen in the leather case which was pinned to her blouse, and she spoke this greeting: "How are you, Nuncle Silas. It's long since I've seen you." She thrust out her arched teeth in a smile. "Good-night, now. You must call and see our Richmond establishment."

"Silas," said John, "empty a dose of the medecyne in a cup for me."

"There's little comfort in medecyne," Silas observed. "Not much use is the stuff if the Lord is calling you home. Calling you home. Shall I read you a piece from the Beybile of the Welsh? It is a great pity you have forgot the language of your mother."

"I did not hear you," said John. "Don't you trouble to say it over." He drank the medicine. "Unfortunate was the row about the Mermaid Agency. I was sorry to take it away from you, but if I hadn't some one else would. We kept it in the family, Silas."

"I have prayed a lot," said Silas to his brother, "that me and you are brought together before the day of the death. Nothing can break us from being brothers."

"You are very doleful. I shall shift this little cold."

"Yes-yes, you will. I would be glad to follow your coffin to Wales and look into the guard's van at stations where the train stop, but the fare is big and the shop is without a assistant. Weep until I am sore all over I shall in Capel Shirland Road. When did the doctor give you up?"

"He's a donkey. He doesn't know nothing. Here he is once per day and charging for it. And he only brings his repairs to me."

"The largest charge will be to take you to your blessed home," said Silas. "The railway need a lot of money for to carry a corpse. I feel quite sorrowful. In Heaven you'll remember that I was at your deathbed."

John did not answer.

"Well-well," said Silas, whispering loudly, "making his peace with the Big Man he is"; and he went away, moaning a funereal hymn tune.

John thought over his plight and was distressed, and he spoke to God in Welsh: "Not fitting that you leave the daughter fach alone. Short in her leg you made her. There's a set-back. Her mother perished; and did I complain? An orphan will the pitiful wench be. Who will care for the shop? And the repairing workman? Steal the leather he will. A fuss will be about shop Richmond. Paid have I the rent for one year in advance. Serious will the loss be. Be not of two thinks. Send Lisha to breathe breathings into my inside — in the belly where the heart is. Forgive me that I go to the Capel English. Go there I do for the trade. Generous am I in the collections. Ask the preacher. Take some one else to sit in my chair in the Palace. Amen. Amen and amen." In his misery he sobbed, and he would not speak to Ann nor heed her questionings. At the cold of dawn he thought that Death was creeping down to him, and he screamed: "Allow me to live for a year — two years — and a grand communion set will I give to the Welsh capel in Shirland Road. Individual cups. Silver-plated, Sheffield make. Ann shall send quickly for the price-list."

His fear was such that he would not suffer his beard to be combed, nor have his face covered by a bedsheet; and he would not stretch himself or turn his face upwards: in such a manner dead men lie.

Again came Silas to provoke his brother to his death.

"Richmond shops are letting like anything," he said.

"The place is coming on," replied John. "I was lucky to get one in King's Row. She is cheap too."

"What are you talking about? There's a new boot shop in King's Row already. Next door to the jeweller."

"You are mistook. I have taken her."

"Well, then, you are cheated. Get up at once and make a case. Wear an overcoat and ride in the bus."

But John bade Ann go to Richmond and to say this and that to the owner of the house. Ann went and the house was empty.

A third time Silas came out of Barnes, bringing with him gifts. These are the gifts that he offered his brother John: a tin of lobster, a tin of sardines, a tin of salmon, and a tin of herrings; and through each tin, in an unlikely place, he had driven the point of a gimlet.

"Eat these," he said, "and good they will do you."

"Much obliged," replied John. "I'll try a herring with bread and butter and vinegar to supper. Very much obliged. It was not my blame that we quarrelled. Others had his eye on the agency."

"Tish, I did not want the old Mermaid. You keep her. I got the sole agency for the Gwendoline"

"How is Gwendolines going?"

"More than I can do to keep ztok of her. Four dozen gents' laces and three dozen ladies' ditto on the twenty-fifth, and soon I order another four dozen ladies' buttons."

John called Ann and to her he said: "How is Mermaid ztok?"

"We are almost out of nine gents and four ladies," answered Ann.

"Write Nuncle Silas the order and he'll drop her in the Zity. Pay your fare one way will I, Silas."

Silas fled the next day into the Mermaid warehouse and sought out the manager. "My brother J. Owen and Co. Thornton East has sold his last pair of Mermaids," he said.

He brought trouble into his eyes and made his voice to quiver as he told how that John was dying and how that the shop was his brother's legacy to him. "Send you the goods for this order to my shop in Barnes," he added. "And all future orders. That will be my headquarters."

He did not go to John's house any more; and although John ate of the lobster, the herrings, and the sardines and was sick, he did not die. A week expired and a sound reached him that Silas was selling Mermaid boots; and he enjoined Ann to test the truth of that sound.

"It's sure enough, dad," Ann said.

John's fury tingled. He put on him his clothes and seized a stick, and by the strength of his passion he moved into Barnes; and he pitched himself at the entering in of the shop, and he saw that Ann's speech was right. He came back; and he did not eat or drink or rest until he had removed all that was in his window and had placed therein no other boots than the Mermaids; and on each pair he put a ticket which was truly marked: "Half cost price." On his door he put this notice: "This FIRM has no Connection with the shop in Barnes"; and this notice could be seen and read whether the door was open or shut.

After a period people returned to him, demanding: "I want a pair of Mermaids, please"; and inasmuch as he had no more to sell, they who had dealt with him went to the shop of his brother.

# A WIDOW WOMAN

# A WIDOW WOMAN

THE Respected Davydd Bern-Davydd spoke in this sort to the people who were assembled at the Meeting for Prayer: "Well-well, know you all the order of the service. Grand prayers pray last. Boys ordinary pray middle, and bad prayers pray first. Boys bach just beginning also come first. Now, then, after I've read a bit from the Book of Speeches and you've sung the hymn I call out, Josi Mali will report."

Bern-Davydd ceased his reading, and while the congregation sang, Josi placed his arms on the sill which is in front of pews and laid his head thereon.

"Josi Mali, man, come to the Big Seat and mouth what you think," said Bern-Davydd.

Josi's mother Mali touched her son, whispering this counsel: "Put to shame the last prayer, indeed now, Josi."

By and by Josi lifted his head and stood on his feet. This is what he said: "Asking was I if I was religious enough to spout in the company of the Respected."

"Out of the necks of young youths we hear pieces that are very sensible," said Bern-Davydd. "Come you, Josi Mali, to the saintly Big Seat."

As Josi moved out of the pew, his thick lips fallen apart and his high cheek bones scarlet, his

119

mother said: "Keep your eyes clapped very close, or hap the prayers will shout that you spoke from a hidden book like an old parson."

So Josi, who in the fields and on his bed had exercised prayer in the manner that one exercises singing, uttered his first petition in Capel Sion. He told the Big Man to pardon the weakness of his words, because the trousers of manhood had not been long upon him; he named those who entered the Tavern and those who ate bread which had been swollen by barm; he congratulated God that Bern-Davydd ruled over Sion.

At what time he was done, Bern-Davydd cried out: "Amen. Solemn, dear me, amen. Piece quite tidy of prayer"; and the men of the Big Seat cried: "Piece quite tidy of prayer."

The quality of Josi's prayers gave much pleasure in Sion, and it was noised abroad even in Morfa, from whence a man journeyed, saying: "Break your hire with your master and be a servant in my farm. Wanting a prayer very bad do we in Capel Salem."

Josi immediately asked leave of God to tell Bern-Davydd that which the man from Morfa had said. God gave him leave, wherefore Bern-Davydd, whose spirit waxed hot, answered: "Boy, boy, why for did you not kick the she cat on the backhead?"

Then Josi said to his mother Mali: "A preacher will I be. Go will I at the finish of my servant term to the school for Grammar in Castellybryn."

"Glad am I to hear you talk," said Mali. "Serious pity that my belongings are so few."

"Small is your knowledge of the Speeches," Josi rebuked his mother. "How go they: 'Sell all that you have?' Iss-iss, all, mam fach."

Now Mali lived in Pencoch, which is in the valley about midway between Shop Rhys and the Schoolhouse, and she rented nearly nine acres of the land which is on the hill above Sion. Beyond the furnishings of her two-roomed house, she owned three cows, a heifer, two pigs, and fowls. She fattened her pigs and sold them, and she sold also her heifer; and Josi went to the School of Grammar. Mali laboured hard on the land, and she got therefrom all that there was to be got; and whatever that she earned she hid in a hole in the ground. "Handy is little money," she murmured, "to pay for lodgings and clothes preacher, and the old scamps of boys who teach him." She lived on potatoes and buttermilk, and she dressed her land all the time. People came to remark of her: "There's no difference between Mali Pencoch and the mess in her cowhouse."

Days, weeks, and months moved slowly; and years sped. Josi passed from the School of Grammar to College Carmarthen, and Mali gave him all the money that she had, and prayed thus: "Big Man bach, terrible would affairs be if I perished before the boy was all right. Let you me keep my strength that Josi becomes as large as Bern-Davydd. Amen."

Even so. Josi had a name among Students' College, and even among ordained rulers of pulpits; and Mali went about her duties joyful and glad; it was as if the Kingdom of the Palace of White Shirts was within her. While at her labour she mumbled praises to the Big Man for His goodness, until an awful thought came to her: "Insulting am I to the Large One bach. Only preachers are holy enough to stand in their pray. Not stop must I now; go on my knees will I in the dark."

She did not kneel on her knees for the stiffness that was in her limbs.

Her joy was increased exceedingly when Josi was called to minister unto Capel Beulah in Carmarthen, and she boasted: "Bigger than Sion is Beulah and of lofts has not the Temple two?"

"Idle is your babbling," one admonished her. "Does a calf feed his mother?"

Josi heard the call. His name grew; men and women spoke his sayings one to another, and Beulah could not contain all the people who would hear his word; and he wrote a letter to his mother: "God has given me to wed Mary Ann, the daughter of Daniel Shop Guildhall. Kill you a pig and salt him and send to me the meat."

All that Josi asked Mali gave, and more; she did not abate in any of her toil for five years, when a disease laid hold on Josi and he died. Mali cleaned her face and her hands in the Big Pistil from which you draw drinking water, and she brought forth her black garments and put them on her; and because of her age she could not weep. The day before that her son was to be buried, she went to the house of her neighbour Sara Eye Glass, and to her she said: "Wench nice, perished is Josi and off away am I. Console his widow fach I must. Tell you me that you will milk my cow."

Sara turned her seeing eye upon Mali. "An old woman very mad you are to go two nines of miles."

"Milk you my cow," said Mali. "And milk you her dry. Butter from me the widow fach shall have. And give ladlings of the hogshead to my pigs and scatter food for my hens."

She tore a baston from a tree, trimmed it and blackened it with blacking, and at noon she set forth to the house of her daughter-in-law; and she carried in a basket butter, two dead fowls, potatoes, carrots, and a white-hearted cabbage, and she came to Josi's house in the darkness which is in the morning, and it was so that she rested on the threshold; and in the bright light Mary Ann opened the door, and was astonished. "Mam-in-law," she said, "there's nasty for you to come like this. Speak what you want. Sitting there is not respectable. You are like an old woman from the country."

"Come am I to sorrow," answered Mali. "Boy all grand was Josi bach. Look at him now will I."

"Talking no sense you are," said Mary Ann. "Why you do not see that the house is full of muster? Will there not be many Respecteds at the funeral?"

"Much preaching shall I say?"

"Indeed, iss. But haste about now and help to prepare food to eat. Slow you are, female."

Presently mourners came to the house, and when each had walked up and gazed upon the features of the dead, and when the singers had sung and the Respecteds had spoken, and while a carpenter turned screws into the coffin, Mary Ann said to Mali: "Clear you the dishes now, and cut bread and spread butter for those who will return after the funeral. After all have been served go you home to

Pencoch." She drew a veil over her face and fell to weeping as she followed the six men who carried Josi's coffin to the hearse.

Having finished, Mali took her baston and her empty basket and began her journey. As she passed over Towy Street — the public way which is strewn with stones — she saw that many people were gathered at the gates of Beulah to witness Mary Ann's loud lamentations at Josi's grave.

Mali stayed a little time; then she went on, for the light was dimming. At the hour she reached Pencoch the mown hay was dry and the people were gathering it together. She cried outside the house of Sara Eye Glass: "Large thanks, Sara fach. Home am I, and like pouring water were the tears. And there's preaching." She milked her cows and fed her pigs and her fowls, and then she stepped up to her bed. The sounds of dawn aroused her. She said to herself: "There's sluggish am I. Dear-dear, rise must I in a haste, for Mary Ann will need butter to feed the baban bach that Josi gave her."

# UNANSWERED PRAYERS

# UNANSWERED PRAYERS

WHEN Winnie Davies was let out of prison, shame pressed heavily on her feelings; and though her mother Martha and her father Tim prayed almost without ceasing, she did not come home. It was so that one night Martha watched for her at a window and Tim prayed for her at the door of the Tabernacle, and a bomb fell upon the ground that was between them, and they were both destroyed.

All the days of their life, Tim and Martha were poor and meek and religious; they were cheaper than the value set on them by their cheapeners. As a reward for their pious humility, they were appointed keepers of the Welsh Tabernacle, which is at Kingsend. At that they took their belongings into the three rooms that are below the chapel; and their spirits were lifted up marvellously that the Reverend Eylwin Jones and the deacons of the Tabernacle had given to them the way of life.

In this fashion did Tim declare his blessedness: "Charitable are Welsh to Welsh. Little Big Man, boys tidy are boys Capel Tabernacle."

"What if we were old atheists?" cried Martha.

"Wife fach, don't you send me in a fright," Tim said.

They two applied themselves to their tasks: the woman washed the linen and cleaned the doorsteps and the houses of her neighbours, the man put posters on hoardings, trimmed gardens, stood at the doors of Welsh gatherings. By night they mustered, sweeping the floor of the chapel, polishing the wood and brass that were therein, and beating the cushions and hassocks which were in the pews of the most honoured of the congregation. Sunday mornings Tim put a white india-rubber collar under the Adam's apple in his throat, and Martha covered her long, thin body in black garments, and drew her few hairs tightly from her forehead.

Though they clad and comported themselves soberly Enoch Harries, who, at this day, was the treasurer and head deacon of the chapel, spoke up against them to Eylwin Jones. This is his complaint: "Careless was Tim in the dispatch department, delivering the parcel always to the wrong customers and for why he was sacked. Good was I to get him the capel. Careless he is now also. By twilight, dark, and thick blackness, light electric burns in Tabernacle. Waste that is. Sound will I my think. Why cannot the work be done in the day I don't know."

"You cannot say less," said Eylwin Jones. "Pay they ought for this, the irreligious couple. As the English proverb — 'There's no gratitude in the poor.'"

"Another serious piece of picking have I," continued Harries. "I saw Tim sticking on hoarding. 'What, dear me,' I mumbled between the teeth — I don't speech to myself, man, as usual. The Apostles did, now. They wrote their minds. Benefit for many if I put down my religious thinks for a second New

Testament. What say you Eylwin Jones? Lots of says very clever I can give you — 'is he sticking?' A biggish paper was the black pasting about Walham Green Music Hall. What do you mean for that? And the posters for my between season's sale were waiting to go out."

Rebuked, Tim and Martha left over sinning: and Tim put Enoch Harries' posters in places where they should not have been put, wherefore Enoch smiled upon him.

"Try will I some further," said Tim by and by.

"Don't you crave too much," advised Martha. "The Bad Man craved the pulpit of the Big Man."

"Shut your backhead. Out of school will Winnie be very near now."

"Speak clear."

"Ask Enoch Harries will I to make her his servant."

"Be modest in your manner," Martha warned her husband. "Man grand is Enoch."

"Needing servants hap he does."

"Perhaps, iss; perhaps, no."

"Cute is Winnie," said Tim; "and quick. Sense she has."

Tim addressed Enoch, and Enoch answered: "Blabber you do to me, why for? Send your old female to Mishtress Harries. Order you her to go quite respectable."

Curtsying before Mrs Harries, Martha said: "I am Tim Dafis' wife."

"Oh, really. The person that is in charge of that funny little Welsh chapel." Mrs Harries sat at a table. "Give me your girl's name, age, and names of

129

previous employers for references." Having written all that Martha said, she remarked: "We are moving next week to a large establishment in Thornton East. I am going to call it Windsor. Of course the husband and I will go to the English church. I thought I could take your girl with me to Windsor."

"The titcher give her an excellent character."

"I'll find that out for myself. Well, as you are so poor, I'll give her a trial. I'll pay her five pounds a year and her keep. I do hope she is ladylike."

Martha told Tim that which Mrs Harries had said, and Tim observed: "I will rejoice in a bit of prayer."

"Iss," Martha agreed. "In the parlour of the preacher. They go up quicker."

God was requested by Tim to heap money upon Mrs Harries, and to give Winnie the wisdom, understanding, and obedience which enable one to serve faithfully those who sit in the first pews in the chapel.

Now Winnie found favour in the sight of her mistress, whose personal maid she was made and whose habits she copied. She painted her cheeks and dyed her hair and eyebrows and eyelashes; and she frequented Thornton Vale English Congregational Chapel, where now worshipped Enoch and his wife. Some of the men who came to Windsor ogled her impudently, but she did not give herself to any man. These ogles Mrs Harries interpreted truthfully and she whipped up her jealous rage.

"You're too fast," she chided Winnie. "Look at your blouse. You might be undressed. You are a shame to your sex. One would say you are a

Piccadilly street-walker and they wouldn't be far wrong. I won't have you making faces at my visitors. Understand that."

Winnie said: "I don't."

"You must change, miss," Mrs Harries went on. "Or you can pack your box and go on the streets. Must not think because you are Welsh you can do as you like here."

On a sudden Winnie spoke and charged her mistress with a want of virtue.

"Is that the kind of miss you are!" Mrs Harries shouted. "Where did you get those shoes from?"

"You yourself gave them to me."

"You thief! You know I didn't. They are far too small for your big feet. Come along — let's see what you've got upstairs."

That hour Mrs Harries summoned a policeman, and in due time Winnie was put in prison.

Tim and Martha did not speak to any one of this that had been done to their daughter.

"Punished must a thief be," said Tim. "Bad is the wench."

"Bad is our little daughter," answered Martha.

Sabbath morning came and she wept.

"Showing your lament you are, old fool," cried Tim.

"For sure, no. But the mother am I."

Tim said: "My inside shivers oddly. Girl fach too young to be in jail."

A fire was set in the preacher's parlour and the doors of the Tabernacle were opened. Tim, the Bible in his hands, stepped up to the pulpit his eyes closed in prayer, and as he passed up he stumbled.

Eylwin Jones heard the noise of his fall and ran into the chapel.

"What's the matter?" he cried. "Comic you look on your stomach. Great one am I for to see jokes."

"An old rod did catch my toe," Tim explained.

Eylwin changed the cast of his countenance. "Awful you are," he reproved Tim. "Suppose that was me. Examine you the stairs. Now indeed forget a handkerchief have I for to wipe the flow of the nose. Order Winnie to give me one of Enoch Harries. Handkerchiefs white and smelly he has."

"Ill is Winnie fach," said Martha.

"Gone she has for brief weeks to Wales," Tim added.

In the morning Eylwin came to the Tabernacle.

"Not healthy am I," he said. "Shock I had yesterday. Fancy I do a rabbit from Wales for the goitre."

"Tasty are rabbits," Tim uttered.

"Clap up, indeed," said Martha. "Too young they are to eat and are they not breeding?"

"Rabbits very young don't breed," remarked Eylwin.

"They do," Martha avowed. "Sometimes, iss; sometimes, no. Poison they are when they breed."

"Not talking properly you are," said Eylwin. "Why for you palaver about breeding to the preacher? Cross I will be."

"Be you quiet now, Martha," said Tim. "Lock your tongue."

"Send a letter to Winnie for a rabbit; two rabbits if she is small," ordered Eylwin. "And not see your faults will I."

Tim and Martha were perplexed and communed with each other; and Tim walked to Wimbledon where he was not known and so have his errand guessed. He bought a rabbit and carried it to the door of the minister's house. "A rabbit from Winnie fach in Wales," he said.

"Eat her I will before I judge her," replied Eylwin; and after he had eaten it he said: "Quite fair was the animal. Serious dirty is the capel. As I flap my hand on the cushion Bible in my eloquence, like chimney smoke is the dust. Clean you at once. For are not the anniversary meetings on the sixth Sabbath? All the rich Welsh will be there, and Enoch Harries and the wife of him."

He came often to view Tim and Martha at their labour.

"Fortunate is your wench to have holiday," he said one day. "Hard have preachers to do in the vineyard."

"Hear we did this morning," Tim began to speak.

"In a hurry am I," Eylwin interrupted. "Fancy I do butter from Wales with one pinch of salt in him. Tell Winnie to send butter that is salted."

Martha bought two pounds of butter.

"Mean is his size," Tim grieved.

"Much is his cost," Martha whined.

"Get you one pound of marsherin and make him one and put him on a wetted cabbage leaf."

The fifth Sunday dawned.

"Next tomorrow," said Martha, "the daughter will be home. Go you to the jail and fetch her, and take you for her a big hat for old jailers cut the hair very short."

"No-no," Tim replied. "Better she returns and speak nothing. With no questions shall we question her."

Monday opened and closed.

"Mistake is in your count," Martha hinted.

"Slow scolar am I," said Tim. "Count will I once more."

"Don't you, boy bach," Martha hastened to say. "Come she will."

At the dusk of Friday Eylwin Jones, his goitred chin shivering, ran furiously and angrily into the Tabernacle. "Ho-ho," he cried. "In jail is Winnie. A scampess is she and a whore. Here's scandal. Mother and father of a thief in the house of the capel bach of Jesus Christ. Robbed Mistress Harries she did. Broke is the health of the woman nice as a consequent. She will not be at the anniversary meetings because the place is contaminated by you pair. And her husband won't. Five shillings each they give to the collection. The capel wants the half soferen. Out you go. Now at once."

Tim and Martha were sorely troubled that Winnie would come to the Chapel House and not finding them, would go away.

"Loiter will I near by," said Tim.

"Say we rent a room and peer for her," said Martha.

Thereon from dusk to day either Tim or Martha sat at the window of their room and watched. The year died and spring and summer declined into autumn, when on a moonlit night men flew in machines over London and loosened bombs upon the people thereof.

"Feared am I," said Martha, "that our daughter is not in the shelter." She screamed: "Don't stand there like a mule. Pray, Tim man."

Remembering how that he had prayed, Tim answered: "Try a prayer will I near the capel."

So Martha watched at her window and Tim prayed at the door of the Tabernacle.

# LOST TREASURE

# LOST TREASURE

HERE is the tale that is told about Hugh Evans, who was a commercial traveller in drapery wares, going forth on his journeys on Mondays and coming home on Fridays. The tale tells how on a Friday night Hugh sat at the table in the kitchen of his house, which is in Parson's Green. He had before him coins of gold, silver, and copper, and also bills of his debts; and upon each bill he placed certain monies in accordance with the sum marked thereon. Having fixed the residue of his coins and having seen that he held ten pounds, his mind was filled with such bliss that he said within himself: "A nice little amount indeed. Brisk are affairs."

"Millie," he addressed his wife, "look over them and add them together."

"Wait till I'm done," was the answer. "The irons are all hotted up."

Hugh chided her. "You are not interested in my saving. You don't care. It's nothing to you. Forward, as I call."

"If I sit down," Millie offered, "I feel I shall never get up again and the irons are hotted and what I think is a shame to waste gas like this the price it is."

"Why didn't you say so at the first opportunity? Be quick then. I shan't allow the cash to lay here."

Duly Millie observed her husband's order, and what time she proved that which Hugh had done, she was admonished that she had spent too much on this and that.

"I'm doing all I can not to be extravagant," she whimpered. "I don't buy a thing for my back." Her short upper lip curled above her broken teeth and trembled; she wept.

"But whatever," said Hugh softening his spirit, "I got ten soferens in hand. Next quarter less you need and more you have. Less gass and electric. You don't gobble food so ravishingly in warm weather. The more I save."

Having exchanged the ten pounds for a ten-pound note, remorse seized Hugh. " A son of a mule am I," he said. "Dangerous is paper as he blows. If he blows! Bulky are soferens and shillings. If you lose two, you got the remnants. But they are showy and tempting." He laid the note under his pillow and slept, and he took it with him, secreted on his person, to Kingsend Chapel, where every Sunday morning and evening he sang hymns, bowed under prayer, and entertained his soul with sermons.

Just before departing on Monday he gave the note to Millie. "Keep him securely," he counselled her. "Tell nobody we stock so much cash."

Millie put the note between the folds of a Paisley shawl, which was precious to her inasmuch as it had been her mother's, and she wrapped a blanket over the shawl and placed it in a cupboard. But on Friday she could not remember where she had hidden the note; "never mind," she consoled herself, "it will occur to me all of a sudden."

As that night Hugh cast off his silk hat and his frock coat, he shouted: "Got the money all tightly?"

"Yes," replied Millie quickly. "As safe as in the Bank of England."

"Can't be safer than that. Keep him close to you and tell no one. Paper money has funny ways." Hugh then prophesied that in a year his wealth in a mass would be fifty pounds.

"With ordinary luck, and I'm sure you deserve it because you're always at it, it will," Millie agreed.

"No luck about it. No stop to me. We've nothing to purchase. And you don't. At home you are, with food and clothes and a ceyling above you. Kings don't want many more."

"Yes," said Millie. "No."

Weeks passed and Millie was concerned that she could not find the note, tried she never so hard. At the side of her bed she entreated to be led to it, and in the day she often paused and closing her eyes prayed: "Almighty Father, bring it to me."

The last Friday of the quarter Hugh divided his money in lots, and it was that he had eleven pounds over his debts. "Eleven soferens now," he cried to his wife. "That's grand! Makes twenty-one the first six months of the wedded life."

"It reflects great credit on you," said Millie, concealing her unhappiness.

"Another eighty and I'd have an agency. Start a factory, p'raps. There's John Daniel. He purchases an house. Ten hands he has working gents' shirts for him."

Millie turned away her face and demanded from God strength with which to acquaint her husband of her misfortune. What she asked for was granted unto her at her husband's amorous moment of the Sabbath morning.

Hugh's passion deadened, and in his agony he sweated.

"They're gone! Every soferen," he cried. "They can't all have gone. The whole ten." He opened his eyes widely. " Woe is me. Dear me. Dear me."

Until day dimmed and night greyed did they two search, neither of them eating and neither of them discovering the treasure.

Therefore Hugh had not peace nor quietness. Grief he uttered with his tongue, arms, and feet, and it was in the crease of his garments. He sought sympathy and instruction from those with whom he traded. "All the steam is gone out of me," he wailed. One shopkeeper advised him: "Has it slipped under the lino?" Another said: "Any mice in the house? Money has been found in their holes." The third said: "Sure the wife hasn't spent it on dress. You know what ladies are." These hints and more Hugh wrote down on paper, and he mused in this wise: "An old liar is the wench. For why I wedded the English? Right was mam fach; senseless they are. Crying she has lost the yellow gold, the bitch. What blockhead lost one penny? What is in the stomach of my purse this one minute? Three shillings — soferen — five pennies — half a penny — ticket railway. Hie backwards will I on Thursday on the surprise. No comfort is mine before I peep once again."

He pried in every drawer and cupboard, and in the night he arose and inquired into the clothes his wife had left off; and he pushed his fingers into the holes of mice and under the floor coverings, and groped in the fireplaces; and he put subtle questions to Millie.

"If you'd done like this in a shop you'd be sacked without a ref," he said when his search was over. "We must have him back. It's a sin to let him go. Reduce expenses at once."

Millie disrobed herself by the light of a street lamp, and she ate little of such foods as are cheapest, whereat her white cheeks sunk and there was no more lustre in her brown hair; and her larder was as though there was a famine in the country. If she said to Hugh: "Your boots are leaking," she was told: "Had I the soferens I would get a pair"; or if she said: "We haven't a towel in the place," the reply was: "Find the soferens and buy one or two."

The more Hugh sorrowed and scrimped, the more he gained; and word of his fellows' hardships struck his broad, loose ears with a pleasant tinkle. While on his journeys he stayed at common lodging-houses, and he did not give back to his employers any of the money which was allowed him to stay at hotels. Some folk despised him, some mocked him, and many nicknamed him "the ten-pound traveller." To the shopkeeper who hesitated to deal with him he whined his loss, making it greater than it was, and expressing: "The interest alone is very big."

By such methods he came to possess one hundred and twenty pounds in two years. His employers had knowledge of his deeds, and they summoned him to them and said to him that because of the drab shabbiness of his clothes and his dishonest acts they had appointed another in his stead.

"You started this," he admonished Millie. "Bring light upon mattar."

"What can I do?" Millie replied. "Shall I go back to the dressmaking as I was?"

Hugh was not mollified. By means of such women man is brought to a penny. He felt dishonoured and wounded. Of the London Welsh he was the least. Look at Enos-Harries and Ben Lloyd and Eynon Davies. There's boys for you. And look at the black John Daniel, who was a prentice with him at Carmarthen. Hark him ordering preacher Kingsend. Watch him on the platform on the Day of David the Saint. And all, dear me, out of J.D.'s Ritfit three-and-sixpence gents' tunic shirts.

He considered a way, of which he spoke darkly to Millie, lest she might cry out his intention.

"No use troubling," he said in a changed manner. "Come West and see the shops."

Westward they two went, pausing at windows behind which were displayed costly blouses.

"That's plenty at two guineas," Hugh said of one.

"It's a Paris model," said Millie.

"Nothing in her. Nothing."

"Not much material, I grant," Millie observed. "The style is fashionable and they charge a lot."

"I like to see you in her," said Hugh. "Take in the points and make her with an odd length of silk."

When the blouse was finished, Hugh took it to a

144

man at whose shop trade the poorest sort of middle-class women, saying: "I can let you have a line like this at thirty-five and six a dozen."

"I'll try three twelves," said the man.

Then Hugh went into the City and fetched up Japanese silk, and lace, and large white buttons; and Millie sewed with her might.

Hugh thrived, and his success was noised among the London Welsh. The preacher of Kingsend Chapel visited him.

"Not been in the Temple you have, Mistar Eevanss, almost since you were spliced," he said. "Don't say the wife makes you go to the capel of the English."

"Busy am I making money."

"News that is to me, Mistar Eevanss. Much welcome there is for you with us."

In four years Hugh had eighteen machines, at each of which a skilled woman sat; and he hired young girls to sew through buttons and hook-and-eyes and to make button-holes. These women and girls were under the hand of Millie, who kept count of their comings and goings and the work they performed, holding from their wages the value of the material they spoilt and of the minutes they were not at their task. Millie laboured faithfully, her heart being perfect with her husband's. She and Hugh slept in the kitchen, for all the other rooms were stockrooms or workrooms; and the name by which the concern was called was "The French Model Blouse Co. Manageress — Mme. Zetta, the notorious French Modiste."

Howsoever bitterly people were pressed, Hugh

did not cease to prosper. In riches, honour, and respect he passed many of the London Welsh.

For that he could not provide all the blouses that were requested of him, he rented a big house. That hour men were arrived to take thereto his belongings, Millie said: "I'll throw the Paisley shawl over my arm. I wouldn't lose it for anything"; and as she moved away the ten-pound note fell on the ground. "Well, I never!" she cried in her dismay. "It was there all the time."

Hugh seized the note from her hand.

"You've the head of a sieve," he said. Also he lamented: "All these years we had no interest in him."

# PROFIT AND GLORY

# PROFIT AND GLORY

BY serving in shops, by drinking himself drunk, and by shamming good fortune, Jacob Griffiths gave testimony to the miseries and joys of life, and at the age of fifty-six he fell back in his bed at his lodging-house in Clapham, suffered, drew up his crippled knees and died. On the morrow his brother Simon hastened to the house; and as he neared the place he looked up and beheld his sisters Annie and Jane fach also hurrying thither. Presently they three saw one another as with a single eye, wherefore they slackened their pace and walked with seemliness to the door. Jacob's body was on a narrow, disordered bed, and in the state of its deliverance: its eyes were aghast and its hands were clenched in deathful pangs.

Then Simon bowed his trunk and lifted his silk hat and his umbrella in the manner of a preacher giving a blessing.

"Of us family can be claimed," he pronounced, "that even the Angel do not break us. We must all cross Jordan. Some go with boats and bridges. Some swim. Some bridges charge a toll — one penny and two pennies. A toll there is to cross Jordan."

"He'll be better when he's washed and laid out proper," remarked the woman of the lodging-house.

149

"Let down your apron from your head," Simon said to her. "We are mourning for our brother, the son of the similar father and mother. You don't think me insulting if I was alone with the corpse. I shan't be long at my religious performance. I am a busy man like you."

The woman having gone, he spoke at Jacob: "Perished you are now, Shacob. You have unravelled the tangled skein of eternal life. Pray I do you will find rest with the restless of big London. Annie and Jane fach, sorrowful you are; wet are your tears. Go you and drink a nice cup of tea in the café. Most eloquent I shall be in a minute and there's hysterics you'll get. Arrive will I after you. Don't pay for tea; that will I do."

"Iss, indeed," said Annie. "Off you, Jane fach. You, Simon, with her, for fear she is slayed in the street. Sit here will I and speak to the spirit of Shacob."

"The pant of my breath is not back" — Jane fach's voice was shrill. "Did I not muster on reading the death letter? Witness the mud sprinkled on my gown."

"Why should you muster, little sister?" inquired Simon.

"Right that I reach him in respectable time, was the think inside me," Jane fach answered. "What other design have I? Stay here I will. A boy, dear me, for a joke was Shacob with me. Heaps of gifts he made me; enough to fill a yellow tin box."

"Generous he was," Simon said. "Hap he parted with all. Full of feeling you are. But useless that we loll here. No odds for me; this is my day in the

City. How will your boss treat you, Annie, for being away without a pass? Angry will your buyer be, I would be in a temper with my young ladies. Hie to the office, Jane. Don't you borrow borrowings from me if you are sacked."

"You are as sly as the cow that steals into clover," Annie cried out. She removed her large hat and set upright the osprey feathers thereon, puffed out her hair which was fashioned in a high pile, and whitened with powder the birth-stain on her cheek. "They daren't discharge me. I'd carry the costume trade with me. Each second you hear, 'Miss Witton-Griffiths, forward,' and 'Miss Witton-Griffiths, her heinness is waiting for you.' In favour am I with the buyer."

"Whisper to me your average takings per week," Simon craved. "Not repeat will I."

After exaggerating her report, Annie said: "You are going now, then."

Jane fach took from a chair a cup that had tea in it, a candlestick — the candle in which died before Jacob — and a teapot, and she sat in the chair. "Oo-oo," she squeaked. "Sorry am I you are flown."

"Stupid wenches you are," Simon admonished his sisters. "And curious. Scandalous you are to pry into the leavings of the perished dead."

Jane fach, whose shoulders were crumped and whose nose was as the beak of a parrot, put forth her head. "The reins of a flaming chariot can't drag me from him. Was he not father to me? Much he handed and more he promised."

"Great is your avarice," Simon declared.

"Fonder he was of me than anyone," Annie

cried. "The birthdays he presented me with dresses — until he was sacked. While I was cribbing, did he not speak well to my buyer? Fitting I stay with him this day."

"I was his chief friend," said Simon. "We were closer than brothers. So grand was he to me that I could howl once more. Iss, I could preach a funeral sermon on my brother Shacob."

Jacob's virtues were truly related. Much had the man done for his younger brother and sisters; albeit his behaviour was vain, ornamenting his person garishly and cheaply, and comporting himself foolishly. Summer by summer he went to Wales and remained there two weeks; and he gave a packet of tea or coffee to every widow who worshipped in the capel, and a feast of tea and currant bread and carraway-seed cake to the little children of the capel.

Wheedlers flattered him for gain: "The watch of a nobleman you carry" and "The ring would buy a field," said those about Sion; "Never seen a more exact fact simily of King George in my life than you," cried spongers in London public houses. All grasped whatever gifts they could and turned from him laughing: "The watch of the fob is brass"; "No more worth than a play marble is the ring"; "Old Griffiths is the bloomin' limit." Yet Jacob had delight in the thought that folk passed him rich for his apparel and acts.

"Waste of hours very awful is this," Simon uttered by and by. He brought out his order book and a blacklead pencil. "Take stock will I now and put down."

He searched the pockets of Jacob's garments

and the drawers in the chest, and knelt on his knees and peered under Jacob's bed; and all that he found were trashy clothes and boots. His sisters tore open the seams of the garments and spread their fingers in the hollow places, and they did not find anything.

"Jewellary he had," exclaimed Annie. "Much was the value of his diamond ring. 'This I will to you,' he said to me. Champion she would seem on my finger. Half a hundred guineas was her worth."

"Where is the watch and chain?" Jane fach demanded. "Gold they were. Link like the fingers of feet the chain had. These I have."

"Lovely were his solitaires," cried Annie. "They are mine."

"Liar of a bitch," said Jane fach. "'All is yours,' mouthed Shacob my brother, who hears me in the Palace."

Simon answered neither yea nor no. He stepped down to the woman of the house. "I have a little list here of the things my brother left in your keeping," he began. "Number wan, gold watch ——"

The woman opened her lips and spoke: "Godstruth, he didn't have a bean to his name. Gold watch! I had to call him in the mornings. What with blacking his whiskers and being tender on his feet, which didn't allow of him to run to say the least of it, I was about pretty early. Else he'd never get to Ward's at all. And Balham is a long run from here."

"I will come back and see you later," Simon replied, and he returned to his sisters. "Hope I do," he said to them, "you discover his affairs. All belong to you. Tall was his regard for you two. Now we will prepare to bury him. Privilege to bury the

153

dead. Sending the corpse to the crystal capel. Not wedded are you like me. Heavy is the keep of three children and the wife."

"For why could not the fool have saved for his burying, I don't say?" Annie cried. "Let the perished perish. That's equal for all."

"In sense is your speech," Simon agreed. "Shop fach very neat he might have if he was like me and you."

"Throwing away money he did," Annie said. "I helped him three years ago when he was sacked. Did I not pay for him to sleep one month in lodgings?"

"I got his frock coat cleaned at cost price," Jane fach remembered, "and sewed silk on her fronts. I lent him lendings. Where are my lendings?"

"A squanderer you were," Simon rebuked the body. "Tidy sums you spent in pubs. Booze got you the sack after twenty years in the same shop. Disgraced was I to have such a brother as you, Shacob. Where was your religion, man? But he has to be buried, little sisters, or babbling there'll be. Cheap funeral will suit in Fulham cematary. Reasonable your share is more than mine, because the Big Man has trusted me with sons."

"No sense is in you," Annie shouted. "Not one coin did he repay me. The coins he owed me are my share."

"As an infidel you are," said Simon. "Ach y fy, cheating the grave of custom."

"Leaving am I." Jane fach rose. "Late is the day."

"Woe is me," Simon wailed. "Like the old

Welsh of Cardigan is your cunning. Come you this night here to listen to funeral estimates. Don't you make me bawl this in your department, Annie, and in your office laundry, Jane."

From the street door he journeyed by himself to Balham, and habiting his face with grief, he related to Mr Ward how Jacob died.

"He passed in my arms," he said; "very gently — willingly he gave back the ghost. A laugh in his face that might be saying: 'I see Thy wonders, O Lord.'"

"This is very sad," said Mr Ward. "If there is anything we can do ——"

"You speak as a Christian who goes to chapel, sir. It's hard to discuss business now just. But Jacob has told he left a box in your keep."

"I don't think so. Still, I'll make sure." Mr Ward went away, and returning, said: "The only thing he left here is this old coat which he wore at squadding in the morning. Of course there is his salary ——"

"Yes, yes, I know. I'd give millions of salaries for my brother back."

"You are his only relative?"

"Indeed, sir. No father and mother had he. An orphan. Quite pathetic. I will never grin again. Good afternoon, sir. I hope you'll have a successful summer sale."

"Hadn't you better take his money?" said Mr Ward. "We pay quarterly here."

"Certainly it will save coming again. But business is business, even in the presence of the dead."

"It's eighteen pounds. That's twelve weeks at one-ten."

"Well, if you insist, insist you do. Prefer I would to have my brother Jacob back."

Simon put the coat over his arm and counted the money, and after he had drunk a little beer and eaten of bread and cheese, he made deals with a gravedigger and an undertaker, and the cost for burying Jacob was eight pounds.

That night he was with his sisters, saying to them: "Twelve soferens will put him in the earth. Four soferens per each."

"None can I afford," Jane fach vowed. "Not paid my pew rent in Capel Charing Cross have I."

"Easier for me to fly than bring the cash," said Annie. "Larger is your screw than me."

Simon smote the ground with his umbrella and stayed further words. "Give the soferens, bullocks of Hell fire."

Annie and Jane fach were distressed. The first said: "The flesh of the swine shall smell before I do." The second said: "Hard you are on a bent-back wench."

Notwithstanding their murmurs, Simon hurled at them the spite of his wrath, reviling them foully and filthily; and the women got afraid that out of his anger would come mischief, and each gave as she was commanded.

The third day Simon and Annie and Jane fach stood at Jacob's grave; and Annie and Jane were put to shame that Simon bragged noisily how that he had caused a name-plate to be made for Jacob's coffin and a wreath of glass flowers for the mound of Jacob's grave.

APPENDIX

Two Deleted Stories

WISDOM

# WISDOM

In his thirty-fifth year David Rees engaged himself to marry Ada Morris. That was when his house-keeper expressed to him her sorrow that at a certain month childbirth would tarnish her glory, whence her name would be as evil as a thirty-pounds with a latch-key shop girl.

"Miss Shones fach," David whispered, "don't you be so loud."

"Hoity-toity! One salted herring I do not care."

Though David charged her with having given herself to men, ordered her to leave his house, and spoke to her of a woman in Pimlico and a doctor in Islington, Tilly laughed at his spleen and was heedless of his advice.

Over that night he kept the door of his bedroom locked, in the fear that Tilly would come to him and provoke him to further ill. Reflecting that his debts were higher than his ownings, he thought out plans to hinder his servant from saying this and that to his discredit. Solemn bad would be affairs if Isaac Morris heard. Come would the flat-bellied, bandy-legged, red-eared lout from his bricks and mortar and spit the spittle of his angry churning on the floor and stock of the shop fach; and he would shout: "Keep the two thousand will I in the pocket and the wench shall marry another."

Subduing his rage and colouring his alarm, he tried to soothe Tilly.

"Be you reasonable," he said. "Do rightly will I and settle your expenses. Fine will the ref be that I will give you."

"They'll cut me out of capel," Miss Jones sobbed. "But scream out will I first."

"Home is best for you, dear heart. Take you a curtain ring and tell a soldier is the husband. At the bettering of trade fetch you will I. Drop dead if I don't."

"Wed me now before I begin to show up."

"A bankrupt will I be if the business don't improve."

David pushed up the shutters of the two windows of the Bon Marche and opened the doors; and thereon he and his three women assistants attended to such as came to custom. Throughout the day he was perplexed, and at the end of the day his spirit was very low.

"Fifty pounds I give you," he announced to Miss Jones. "Run in the train."

Tilly fixed a sailor hat slantwise on her head and drew a veil over her face, the freckles on which were like rosebuds.

"Meeting for prayer there is in Capel King's Cross," she hinted.

"Too late you are. Not made the supper of the young ladies you have."

"Meet the persons at the door I must."

"Well, ho. Go you," said David.

Miss Jones departed, and he journeyed to the public house in which the men of Capel King's

Cross make themselves drunk after prayer, and albeit he asked dark questions, none nicknamed him improperly nor accused him.

In the kitchen of the Bon Marche he spoke smartly to Miss Jones. "One hundred soferens is my last offer and I've had nothing to do with your child."

"Twice times that I want, David Rees."

"Said my say I have and say no more I say and one hundred soferens is five shillings per week for eight years."

"Tut-tut, stay here will I."

"Headstiff against your interests you are, female," cried David.

Tilly tempted him: she loosened her yellow hair, unhooked her skirt and took off her blouse, and she sat in a chair and threw back her head.

David fell.

Early in the morning one stirred the other, and Miss Jones went away with her belongings and two hundred pounds; and David married Ada, with the money of whose father Isaac he enlarged the Bon Marche.

In his marriage David acted wisely and prosperity came to him. What hours the doors were not closed either he or Ada was in the shop. The two ate meals separately and they took each other's counsel in all things. Every Saturday they counted their outgoings and incomings, and always one of them said: "We have so much more than we had last week." Sundays they spent at Capel King's Cross, where they were honoured for their wealth and their faithfulness. To each other they were more than what men are to women; they were what men are to men.

Eight years after their marriage a sickness seized Isaac; he willed all that he had to his son-in-law and died.

Ada and David feigned deep grief. They had a narrow black board put on each of the fifteen windows of the Bon Marche and for twelve months they preserved the habits of the grieved in Capel King's Cross. Yet they consoled themselves: "Fullish was his life and very saving."

In the company of the most high men of the Capel David splayed his feet and boasted of his good fortune.

"How many children have you, man?" one asked him slyly.

"Hap you need help, boy bach," an old man wheezed. "Assister quite brisk am I."

"Work while the day is on," David replied, "then children."

"Rees! Rees!" the old man said. "A rabbit of a brain you have. The Gospel does not say of the night."

David pondered. The business had grown. It was the biggest in Kentish Town, and the number of employees was above one hundred and five. People bach, there's a wonder! Put Isaac's money he will in a new shop, and the name over the shop shall be that of his first baban bach.

Weeks and months passed and David addressed his wife Ada: "No understanding is in me. Healthy me and you are."

He inquired of a physician, and the physician

instructed Ada to go from the Bon Marche, and to abide in a house in Hampstead. David obeyed, and he bought Astolat, which is in Downshire Drive; but Ada remained as she was. The physician made a further inquisition of the matter, and he said: "A small operation and you'll be all right."

Ada crawled down from her bed and halted abroad with the indecision of a woman who has rarely recovered her senses; the bags of her eyes were limpid and the light in her eyes was thick and turpid.

David nursed his patience and then, full of misery, sent up a plea to God. He also put arguments in the mouth and money in the hand of a preacher, and the preacher bade God multiply the Welsh nation and to listen to the cry of His religious little children.

"I've done my bit," the preacher reported to David. "Now you perform. Or would you like me to perform for you, man?"

As God did not make any sign, David's longing brewed into fierce revolt against preachers, his wife, Capel King's Cross, and God.

"If you'd married somebody else," he reproached Ada, "you'd have them right enough."

"Is this my blame?" Ada uttered.

"Of course. And after all I've paid on you. The operation was cash down. You're not a woman, for serious. As the flesh of a cow you would only be fit for the assistants." He did not speak kindly to Ada again. Soon after, one shook him, saying: "Mrs Rees is dead. She died in her sleep." He shaved the folds of his sagging chin, put on him black clothes, ate, and went to his shop.

A shopwalker opened for him a door and gaped despondingly.

"Yes, mistar?" David cried.

The man placed his palms together and crooked his right leg, and he began to speak: "I wish on this sad occasion to most respectfully offer my condolants. The Great Reaper —"

"Who gave orders for the blinds down?" David interrupted.

"As a sign of the respect we one and all feel to the sacred dead, I thought —"

"Like the gaze of them, eh, mistar? Take your bloody box and sit on it and gaze on them. Clear out this minute. And don't apply to me for a ref. Hay, miss, pull up the blinds."

David repented the twenty-three years he was harnessed to a sterile woman, and neither his bitterness nor his desire would be appeased. There was no one to whom he could give the secret of his might, no one who would cry out: "Father bach made this what she is," none of whom it could could be written: "and son."

He cast off his gloom as on the morrow of Ada's funeral he had cast off the mourning which concealed his gladness. "Wed once more will I," he vowed. "And dear me, try the wench will I first." He would cheat Nature: he reddened his moustaches and the sparse hairs which were on the nape of his neck, and he had false teeth fixed behind his hanging lips; thus he tricked his imaginings into the belief that the strength of youth was within him.

Fathers and mothers heard of his designs and

urged their daughters to trade at the Bon Marche; and David courted a few and dealt gallantly by all: "for," he said, "this is a nice adfertyzement". Now of those he wooed Emma Pryce was more in his sight than all the others. With her he went here and there.

"Everything I got," he lamented to her, "but children."

"That's a sad pity," observed Emma.

"It's never too late to repair."

"And you're so fond of them," said Emma. "What a tragedy."

Immediately Emma became as the mistress of Astolat: she directed David in his speech and what he wore. On the dining room wall, above the brass horn of the gramophone, she hung a picture of him set in a great gilt frame and on its left a picture of the Bon Marche as it was in the beginning, and on its right of the Bon Marche as it was then; and under the three she put a strip of polished mahogany on which this phrase was printed: "David Rees the Welsh Merchant Prince". The three servants she sent away, for that they disregarded her orderings and tattled impudently of her, and she chose others in their places. She did as seemed fitting to her in everything and was given whatsoever she wanted; she adorned her hands with Ada's rings, her ears with Ada's jewels, her neck with Ada's pearls.

Gladness was brought into the life of David Rees. When he willed Emma's arms opened for him, and lips, between which teeth gleamed like white pebbles sunk in burnt clay, smiled at him.

At the setting in of winter he arrayed Emma in a sealskin coat and to the high men of Capel King's Cross he said: "This is the future Messes Rees."

The high men answered: "Congratulations, now"; apart from him they said: "A piece very warm is Rees Bon Marche. Is he not always opening shop?"

But he could not sleep for the questionings of his inclination. Old age was near him. Death waited under the counter, licking his whetstone. Ada's first children would be arriving at manhood now.... The portion of the maid's bridal seeds are mixed up with the husband's portion, and the fulness of the shootings therefrom is astonishing. Tilly's child was twenty-three, and he was of the bridal sowing.

Beneath the dye, his hairs were white. Youth should beget; old age should frolic, inasmuch as it begets only weaklings.

This is what he said to Emma: "Leave me until we are wedded. Babblers are adding two and four and talking"; and of this he was afraid: "Hap the child of Matilda is an old fool."

He went down into Morfa, which is in Cardigan Bay; and one answered his question: "Perished is Tilly fach, for sure me."

"You don't say, poor female," David remarked.

"Boy chance she had and perished. Cobbler clogs is Dai bach her boy chance."

David hastened to his son's house — which is of two rooms and below the pigstyes and cowhouses of Pant — and he stepped through the mess that was gathered before the door.

"Is this the place of Dai cobbler?" he asked.

"Why for you don't walk silent?" cried Dai rebukingly. "Startled the hens from their nests you have. Egg in hedges they will. Here's awful loss." He scattered corn on his bed and under his bed. "Come back, hens fach. Clook. Clook-clook."

"Hurtful is the sole of the boot," said David. "Ease her."

"Too busy am I, little stranger."

"Do you this for me."

"Without a belly you are to stop my work." Dai examined the boot. "Cheap she is. One silver shilling is the price."

"Biggish is your charge."

"Take her off, man. Not wishing to do your bad boot do I."

"Pay you will I then," said David.

"From where you are?" asked Dai.

"Male from London."

"Don't be slow, seeing how busy I am. What are you called?"

"David Rees."

"A preacher you are? Be quick and say your affairs."

David answered his son, who then said: "Fair day."

Three times did David prove Dai's wisdom, and on the fourth day he made himself known.

"A close black you are, father bach," replied Dai.

So Dai collected the money that was due to him and sold his hens and all that was his, and he cleansed his feet and face in the pond of Pant; and he was brought to London to his father's house.

Of this that was done, David did not tell Emma, nor did he seek her out, and he commanded a servant to say to her: "The master is not in." Emma was puzzled and sent letters inquiring what it was and why it was; David answered them not. In the spring of the year Emma wrote of her shame to go abroad and prayed for a speedy marriage. The letter David interpreted to his son, who cried: "What's the matter with the female? Mouth you to her that your boy Dai bach is here."

Even so.

# THE LANTERN BEARER

# THE LANTERN BEARER

Twenty-five years ago, when he was employed at Master's World Stores, Enoch Harries had a mind to own a drapery shop. He put his trust in Rhys Hopkins, adding: "What say you to partners?"

He spoke in Welsh and therefore in secret, for none but they two of the eight men who slept in the apartment had knowledge of Welsh.

"Good that will be", Rhys replied. "Glad am I."

A little later Enoch said: "Found her have I in Kingsend. Busy neighbourhood that is and close to Putney and Walham Green. Collect, dear me, our money for the shop fach. Shop very fach she will be at the first forever."

Rhys caused to be sold the sixteen acres of land by which his mother lived in Carmarthenshire; and the sum of money that he gave to Enoch was nearly two hundred pounds.

He was pious and laborious: singing hymns as he swept the floor, dusted the counter or shelves, dressed the window or overhead brass rods; breathing praises to the God who helped him to falsify measures and money to his advantage. Enoch, mindful of all that Rhys did, thought in this wise: "Draper first-rate he is. Have him out I must less he plays the high arm against me." So he wrote lying figures in a book and assuming anguish and distress, showed these figures to Rhys.

"Horrid are affairs, Enoch bach," said Rhys, having mused upon them.

"Terrible for sure," Enoch moaned. "Nasty bit of disgrace is coming to us."

"For why did you trick me of the money of mam fach, you boar? Lost all has dear mam."

"Considered that have I. Forgive you then. Rid you yourself at once and swallow the hard pill will I alone."

With one hundred and ten pounds Rhys withdrew. He bought a milk walk; and though he stayed pious and laborious, he let his passions move wantonly. Soon he could not pay his bills, and he sought Harries, who pitied him and made him a shopwalker, appointing him a wage of thirty pounds a year, beyond his food and lodging. The concern had grown and many men and women were engaged in its conduct.

All that Rhys did pleased Enoch, and he was set over that prayer meeting which is held in the half hour before the shop is opened.

On a Thursday in June it fortuned that Enoch got up early to join his workpeople in asking God's blessing on his summer sale, and behold fifteen of his assistants were not in view. Enoch lifted his head and allowed anger to redden his cheeks; and his tongue stammered as he rated those who were present for those who were not there.

Then he shouted to Rhys: "I thought I told you, mister, that everybody must attend prayers. You don't think of nobody but you, man. And as well the sale commences Monday morning nine hae hem

sharp. It means I have to order more window plac-
ards. They ought to be taken out of your screw."

"Like this it happened ——" Rhys began to
answer.

"Don't prevaricake. Do as you are obliged, or
off you go. I picked you down from the gutter. The
clothes you are wearing was bought with my pocket. In future everyone who are not at prayer they
shall be fined one shilling and two-and-six for the
second time and a minute's notice without a ref for
the third. I will not have atheists in my shop."

Faithfully Rhys did as he was commanded, and
at the end of a period Enoch made a count of the
levy thus got, and the levy he gave to the Building
Fund of Kingsend Welsh Tabernacle. Rhys was
again preferred; to his duties was added that of
overseer of staff: at a quarter-past-eleven he went
into bedrooms to ensure that no light was burning,
and at certain periods of the day he went into the
lavatories to hasten any such as loitered therein.

Once on his round he bantered a young woman
who slept alone in a room; the next night he dark-
ened his lantern and sat upon her bed. In the spring
of the morning he went to his own bed. Presently
the young woman could not give attendance to
prayers.

"You'll get into trouble," Rhys warned her.

"Perhaps I'm in trouble," the woman replied.

"I'll have to run you in. Can't help myself."

"I can say something too. You're a fine one to
call me to pray."

The more Rhys thought on what he had done
the more afraid he became; and he spoke to the

woman's damage to Harries: that her speech was lewd, that she was a whore and a thief.

"I don't care what she does after bizness," said Harries. "I won't have thieves here. Trap her. I'll have the bitch locked up. I'll learn them to steal from me."

"I've tried to catch her," said Rhys. "She knows we are watching her. Kick her out."

Then Rhys urged on his lust; he peered over and under the doors of the women's lavatories, he fingered the discarded calico garments which were in his way as he passed with his lantern, his imagination magnifying the value of the trumpery things that were hidden from him.

He did not meddle any more with the women in Harries' Store; he trafficked with the women who hawked their favours in the streets, dallying with them in doorways and at the mouths of dark alleys.

In his forty-fifth year there were sores in his body and his stride was as the stride of a gouty man; and he was an offence unto those who came by him.

The head woman of the costume department complained to Harries: "You see, it isn't right. See what I mean. And his nasal organ and whiskers are nice things for young ladies to look on, I'm sure. If you understand what I mean. The other young ladies object too. He don't stop scratching hisself. Really, Mr Harries, he is not fit to be with young shop ladies. Especially showroom young ladies. You'll excuse me, Mr Harries."

"Most certain, miss. I am busy now just."

"Baths are cheap enough. All us young showroom ladies go every Friday night to Portland Road

Baths — all us who can go. Being a married man, Mr Harries, you'll pardon me for mentioning intimated instincts."

Harries upraided Rhys and gave his offices to another; and he lowered his wage by fifteen pounds and sent him to labour and to eat with the porters.

The man washed his body but did not abandon his pursuits. His lust was costlier than his earnings, and he paid for the quenching of it with pilferings from the shop. His practice came to the ear of Harries, who rebuked him, took him before a magistrate, brought women to bear witness against him, and had him put in prison. He was let free at the spring cribbing and he mingled with the cribbers at the doors of shops; but engagers remembered his misdemeanour and bade him begone.

He implored God to blot out his fault and of such was his faith that this answer reached him: "Ask the forgiveness, little pig, of the boy bach you robbed. Serious thing to take goods from stock without paying."

Rhys obeyed.

"Doing very bad am I", said Harries, "to give you five shillings considering your stealings. Starve would I before breaking my character."

"Lesson very awful was I teached."

"Spend you the five shillings in the baby department on pins and needles and bootlaces and collar studs and hooks-and-eyes and sell same honestly. Recall my charity when you want more and buy them here. Tell you all that the male you defrauded gives you the second start in life."

Rhys peddled; to the people who opened the

doors to him, he said: "I am not an ordinary tramp. I've been greatly well-off. This is me: taken in frock coat and silk hat. I gave ten-and-six for the umberellar, which was cost price." As he walked he sang: "Jesus, Jesus, you sufficeth; greater than the world you are."

In such a manner Rhys Hopkins lived: peddling, singing, praying. Howsoever hard he asked to be raised in the sight of man and howsoever deep in his heart was the fear of God, yet Satan prompted him to perform to the hurt of his welfare.

"Not in the right tone can my prayers be," he said. "Copy Harries I must. Full of eloquence he is and plentiful blessings he has had."

He entered Harries' Store by stealth and secreted himself overnight in the garret that is over the room in which Harries prays in the presence of his men and women; and in the morning he heard Harries praying, and he saw the words of the prayer coming through the floor in the shape of a spider's thread. The thread floated this way and that way before it cleaved to the walls and roof of the garret.

Rhys was concerned for the soul of Harries and he ran down to him and cried: "There's a stock of prayers, man, you've got in the garret. You must change their form if you want them to go higher."

"Fetch the poliss," Harries shouted. "Tell them a bergular is on the premizez."

For two years after he was released Rhys limped hither and thither, treading softly up to people and whispering: "You're on the road to Hell", standing on the wayside and crying: "I am the son of God." He was the laughing-stock of the mocker and the gazing-stock of the curious. His bed he made in the midst of a thick growth which is in Palewell Park.

Before the twilight of a day he drank of the well that is by a pathway; and as he sucked he saw his likeness in the water.

"Not the face of man do I see," he cried. "The face of Jesus bach is here and the face is me"; and he put a cheek at the surface of the water. "Iss," he answered, "say will I that I am Jesus. Start will I at once."

At the turn-gate he met an old woman.

"I am Jesus Christ," he announced.

The woman was for passing him by, for she knew that he had nothing to give her.

"Pray to Jesus," said Rhys.

The woman's hand fell from her bodice, and the garment parted and revealed the waste of her breasts.

"I feel I'm dying," she said.

"Then confess quickly. Death is a serious affair if you don't repent."

"Perhaps a rest will pull me together," the woman murmured.

"Why talk about dying then to a man in a hurry? But I will show you a place. Come now."

Rhys led the woman to the wild growth, and as he bent the twigs for her to enter, he said: "Cover your body with the sacks. Good night."

In the morning darkness he rose and went into the growth and he lay at the side of the woman and he put a hand on her bosom.

"How are we going on?" he said. "Two's

warmer than one."

At the first singing of the birds he awoke and stretched himself; and on his knees he told God that a woman had tempted him even as Eve had tempted Adam bach.

"Sataness," he cried rising to his feet, "go off."

None answered him. The woman had died with the night.

# Afterword

*My Neighbours* (1920) was the final yield of the great creative outburst that began, sensationally, with *My People* (1915), Evans's fifteen stories of greed, cunning and cruelty, set in a south Cardiganshire village maddened by oppressive religion. Twelve months later *Capel Sion* fixed the author's twofold reputation: that of daring literary original (in subject matter and style) and the betrayer of Wales, a homeland he had traduced in exchange for English gold. By spring 1917 more immediate difficulties faced him. As editor of *Ideas*, a popular penny weekly, he had become embroiled in the sex-and-spies scandal surrounding a Mayfair socialite, a woman eventually deported as an undesirable alien active in German espionage. Convinced that high-level friends had protected her, he laid the charge of an establishment cover-up, of misdeeds in "frowsy Bohemia, where men of the great world meet women of the half-world". With a libel action brewing, Edward Hulton, his alarmed proprietor, settled expensively out of court and Evans was handed his cards. It came as no surprise; this was rich man's justice, the only kind there could be. As he wrote on the eve of dismissal, "The humble shall serve the boastful; the rich shall be as gods, and they shall do no wrong, for the laws will be in their keeping."

Fleet Street editorial pressures did not stem the creative flow. In 1917 he published four stories, two in the

*Saturday Westminster Gazette*, an influential evening newspaper with Naomi Royde-Smith as its literary editor. Part-Welsh, greatly talented, the muse of Walter de la Mare, she gave her readers a chance to sample "a satirist of his own people unmatched in English literature since Swift". He did not disappoint. "A Widow Woman" maps the fate of a humble, self-sacrificing widow who ominously prays that her son be "as large as Bern-Davydd", the minister of Capel Sion. A second front-page story, "Treasure and Trouble", has a victimised farmer driven to suicide by the brutal greed of his brother, a noise in Bern-Davydd's chapel. Evans's creativity was invariably triggered by real-life events, in this case a hanging at Rhydlewis, his boyhood home. As he explained elsewhere, it pointed the depths of docility and passive suffering that religious government could induce (and an independent witness, while not mentioning that the farmers were brothers, confirms that in disputes of this kind chapel factions often took sides).

For the *English Review*, the journal that was first to recognise his literary gifts, Evans chose a story with a London setting. In "Earthbred" (1918) his city émigrés scheme over a dairy business as they might have over a farm, employing pretence and evasion to gauge or falsify its worth; remarkably, the story proceeds almost entirely through dialogue, of the oblique, distrustful kind perfected in *Capel Sion*. "Joseph's House", also given to the *English Review*, shows Evans at his best ("the beautiful clear-cut simplicity of the story is a joy," wrote Rhys Davies to the writer and editor Gwyn Jones). Here Evans more fully inhabits the consciousness of his characters, their peculiar precepts and pieties, twisted notions of morality, occasional loving deceits. There is pathos in their trapped condition, and an affecting reciprocal tenderness between Madlen and

Joseph her son as they meet the inevitable. "There's silly, dear people, to covet houses! Only a smallish bit of house we want." Madlen's words allude to Penlan cottage, and to Joseph's burial spot; to the coffin that London colleagues deemed his only proper purchase.

*Who's Who* for 1919 signalled Evans's public arrival. His entry confirmed his address as 26 Thornton Road, East Sheen, on the Surrey outskirts of London. "Walking in London" was his listed recreation; he might have added, "and writing about the London Welsh", for by now the basilisk gaze had fully fallen on his metropolitan neighbours. Many were honoured names, thriving in the commercial kingdom. "Moreover, people, look you at John Lewis. Study his marble gravestone in the burial ground of Capel Sion: 'His name is John Newton-Lewis; Paris House, London, his address. From his big shop in Putney, Home they brought him by railway.'" Numbering some forty thousand, the London Welsh were present in most trades and professions, though thickest in drapery and the dairy trade. Evans's own Cardiganshire kinsfolk had cornered the milk rounds, in the suburbs and in the city, where they sold their pints and pats of butter along Fleet Street. His compatriots banded together, living a life in some ways as Welsh as that lived in Wales. Their paper, *The London Welshman*, reveals both sides of an inward-looking community, a touchy defensiveness, alert to the smallest slight (army discrimination against Welsh officers?), and a bolstering calendar of self-celebration — concerts, rallies, eisteddfodau, Cymmrodorion and St David's Day festivities. There were intellectual circles too, notably the Friday evening salon of Mary Ellis, wife of Ellis Jones Griffith, Anglesey Liberal MP. "There is all the difference", reflected the writer Wyn Griffith, "between discussing cultural issues in a cold

185

chapel vestry, and a gathering such as this, which contributed to our social awareness as well as our knowledge of the arts." Fleet Street sharpened Evans's social awareness — not least of Liberal MPs — while for literary company he had Arthur Machen and fellow journalists in the pubs off Ludgate Circus. "When we meet in taverns we fall to quarrelling about Welsh pronunciation," wrote Machen in June 1919; "the Saxons about us think the strange words must be German and look at us suspiciously, and on one occasion, an *Evening News* colleague, who was sitting with Caradoc and myself, called out in a loud voice: 'Intern them all!'"

If Evans loved the tavern spirit ("the same lads in the same place at the same time"), so he did his "sermon-tasting"; and chapel going as much as drapery gave him bearings on the London Welsh. He savoured the toothsome dramatics of Welsh pulpit giants, Ben's models at College Carmarthen ("According to the Pattern): "now he was Pharaoh wincing under the plagues, now he was the Prodigal Son longing to eat at the pig's trough, now he was the Widow of Nain rejoicing at the recovery of her son, now he was a parson in Nineveh squirming under the prophecy of Jonah." His delight in the manner of preachers, whom on other grounds he would condemn, understandably intrigued Arthur Machen. His "very turbulent, highly entertaining" companion joined him one evening, following a narrow escape in the suburbs where a famous preacher was performing. "It was lucky I thought of it and had a couple of pints or he would have got me," Caradoc explained. For most of his life a chapelgoer, Christian-spirited, though anti-clerical, in his polemics, Evans confessed himself "a bit of a puritan, a bit of an atheist, a bit of a pagan", and Welsh in his love of the word. As for the heavenly afterlife, "I do not imagine there is anything after death except peace and quiet and a hole in the ground," a late journal entry records.

Evans places his fictional neighbours in his own London patch, the "Thornton East" neighbourhood. This, and some dominant presences, helps integrate a collection lacking *Capel Sion's* tight focus. Evans opts for a broader canvass, embracing community leaders (a preacher-politician, a prosperous draper — "there's boys for you") and those at the bottom of the pile. Ministers figure sparingly, though if *My Neighbours* has a physical centre, it is Eylwin Jones's Kingsend Tabernacle — the "funny little Welsh chapel" rejected by Gwen Enos-Harries for a "Thornton Vale" English equivalent. (Evans here has Sheen Vale Congregational Church in mind, a stone's throw from Thornton Road and sometime in the care of H. Elwyn Thomas, whose Barrie-inspired Welsh novels gave point to his sermons on "novel reading — help or hindrance to the higher life?") In *I Take This City* (1933), his sparkling first impressions of London, the young Welsh journalist Glyn Roberts depicts the queues for Sunday evening services at the larger London-Welsh chapels (King's Cross, Charing Cross, Jewin in the City); two hours later the crowds spill out for pavement chat, kid gloves and black bowlers much in evidence. These chapels, big or small (some thirty-four in all — Evans gave a reader a guinea for listing them), "stand for everything which signifies anything to the draper and the dairyman — home, religion, friendship, the language, music. Within their means and within reason, they will contribute lavishly to the upkeep and smartening of their houses of worship, which are usually glistening and varnished to the nth degree."

"Home, religion, friendship, the language", these are themes in *My Neighbours*. Home is Wales — a good

187

country to come from but not much of a place to live in, as the saying goes. The Welsh worship Home from afar, and like Jacob Griffiths ("Profit and Glory"), they visit it as lordly almoners. "Summer by summer he went to Wales and remained there two weeks; and he gave a packet of tea or coffee to every widow who worshipped in the capel, and a feast of tea and currant bread and car-away-seed cake to the little children of the capel." Back in London, his sister Annie, now Miss Witton-Griffiths, dons a hat of osprey feathers, her hair piled fashionably high, the "birth stain" on her cheek symbolically whitened. An implied social critique gives weight to Evans's personal histories. For all their nationalist protestations, his London Welsh are culturally confused, despising the ungodly English yet aping their social ways. They puff up their surnames ("the hyphen is the mark of our ambition"), regally christen their houses ("Windsor" in the case of Mrs Enos-Harries), forsake their native language for "classier" English. Evans makes play with the shift between languages as charac-ters align themselves socially or bargain over posses-sions. It matters who are, and where you come from. "Are you Welsh?" asks Evan of the woman whose shop he covets. "That's what people say," Mrs Jenkins replies.

As for religion, Evans's drapers and dairymen adhere to a faith that will secure their entry into heaven, the Palace of White Shirts, that paradise of pulpits, bible-thumping prophets and slap-up chapel teas glimpsed in two of the stories. "We must all cross Jordan," sighs Simon Griffiths in "Profit and Glory"; till then, the profit-and-glory spirit of Calvinism must pre-vail ("the Garden of Aden. That is where commerse began. Didn't Eve buy the apple?"). The moral impera-tive is to thrive and prosper: it's good to be rich; the rich are good. Hugh Evans ("Lost Treasure") loses his money together with his sanity, and thus all standing among the chapel Welsh ("grief... was in the crease of his garments"). Then he triumphs as a hard-nosed capitalist, running up cheap fashions on sweated labour. Money speeds him back into the Kingsend fold, as it uplifted John Daniel, another Carmarthen apprentice: "Watch him on the platform on the Day of David the Saint. And all, dear me, out of J. D.'s Ritfit three-and-sixpence gents' tunic shirts."

By contrast Tim and Martha, Kingsend's caretakers and general dogsbodies, are the lowest of the low, in everyone's eyes and their own ("Unanswered Prayers"). "Charitable are Welsh to Welsh," declares Tim, in what might stand as an ironic epigraph for the entire collection. He and Martha meet death outside the chapel they adore, a quick release from the humiliations heaped upon them by "boys tidy" of this Tabernacle, the exploitative Reverend Jones and the heartless Enoch Harries. Their servant daughter Winnie stirs a fateful jealousy in her mistress, though not before confronting Mrs Enos-Harries with a courage absent in others. She is jailed on a trumped-up charge of theft brought by Mishtress Harries, and there is fine emotional delicacy in Evans's handling of the old couple's anguished reactions. Winnie must surely be punished, her employers can't be mistaken. Even so, Martha weeps:

> *"Showing your lament you are, old fool,"*
> *cried Tim.*
> *"For sure, no. But the mother am I."*
> *Tim said: "My inside shivers oddly. Girl*
> *fach too young to be in jail."*

Elsewhere, greed of wealth transcends all family

ties as once again in this collection husbands and wives, brothers and sisters, parents and children, are locked in hideous combat. To paraphrase Hitchcock, Evans brings murder back into the family, where it belongs. One compelling domestic drama, "Love and Hate", charts the slow poisoning of sisterly love as Olwen seeks to do right by her sister Lizzie and by her own daughter Jennie, a spoilt-brat shop assistant with a know-all cockney partner.

The stories set during wartime evoke no sharp sense of the times; no jaunty patriotism, no gathering despair, no gloom of wartime London. Living and working in London, Evans could scarcely have ignored the war. In 1917 the military camped in Richmond Park, billeting troops in private houses near his own. At Sheen Vale chapel, harvest services were abandoned because of air raids. Air raids are mentioned in *My Neighbours* (one kills Tim and Martha), but in a language that removes all sense of immediacy. As editor of a mass-market paper, Evans regularly commented on wartime conditions — in essence, how at home the poorest were being forced to bear the heaviest burdens — but in his fiction the war is a marginal event. His characters go about their money-making, too engaged in personal battles to bother about the national struggle. "St David and the Prophets" marks the attitude of the wealthy Welsh. "You left on your own accord, didn't you?" asks William Hughes-Jones, big draper and chapel deacon, of a soldier home from the front. "I never take back a hand that leave on their own." In wartime, as in peace, class divisions are unsuppressed, and the chapel positively reinforces them. So a minister greets returning servicemen with talk of civilian sacrifices; the Somme is as nothing compared with the sufferings of a deacon: "Happier still we are to welcome Mister Hughes-Jones to the Big Seat. In the valley of the shadow has Mister Hughes-Jones been. Earnestly we prayed for our dear religious leader."

Satire feeds on specific targets, a group, an occupation, individuals. Evans names living persons. The Reverend Eynon Davies, his old *Western Mail* adversary, is given the lordship of Walham Green, while behind Ben Lloyd looms the most celebrated London Welshman of all, the prime minister David Lloyd George, perhaps by the end of the war the most powerful politician in the world. The Welsh practically deified him — at Rhyl he was introduced as the greatest man since Christ. He was the dream incarnate, the personification of nationhood and faith. At least, of his representative quality Evans had no doubt: "Mr George *is* Welsh Nonconformity," he declared in 1916, still smarting from the attempted ban on *My People*. The book had been swept from the shelves by Cardiff police, an action he attributed directly to Lloyd George, who assuredly loathed Caradoc Evans. "Pride of race belongs to the lowest savage. This man is a renegade," he told the journalist Beverly Baxter.

"I hear his silver voice holding spellbound hundreds of people; I see his majestic forehead and his auburn locks and the strands of his silken moustache." A fortune-teller describes Ben Lloyd to a panting Gwen Enos-Harries in phrases that conjure up Lloyd George at his zenith ("For Better"). Evans wasn't so star-struck; indeed, in "According to the Pattern" he broke authorial cover, his tone of detached neutrality (letting actions speak for themselves), to treat of one fiercely determined Welshman and his calculated assault on the city, a preacher with political ambitions who advances through guile, flattery and grandiloquence, and deems that advancement a mark of God's favour.

191

*He bound himself to Welsh politicians and*
*engaged himself in public affairs, and soon*
*he was an idol to the multitude of people,*
*who were sensible only to his well-sung*
*words, and who did not know that his utter-*
*ances veiled his own avarice and that of his*
*masters. All that he did was for profit, and yet*
*he could not win enough.*

The key to this extraordinary character lay in the Wales
that bred him. "According to the Pattern" has Ben learning from the ministers, progressing through religious
cunning, pulpit fire-and-brimstone, and onslaughts
against Anglican priestcraft. A single sentence on Ben's
father marvellously suggests the standing of women in
this community. A father of seven daughters by a
(nameless) first wife, Abel marries well a second time
(to "the widow of Drefach"). Yet, "Even if Abel had
land, money, and honour, his vessel of contentment was
not filled until his wife went into her deathbed and gave
him a son." This is hallmark Evans, the deep disgust
controlled in prose of lapidary beauty.

Besides mimicking his "well-sung words", Ben's
speeches closely mirror Lloyd George's Welsh concerns
(tithe, temperance, disestablishment, home rule). But it
is the anti-unionism which stands out. Ben is the lost
leader, the one-time champion of the shop workers'
cause who is bought over by the big Welsh drapers.
Now "Fiery Taffy" mocks their struggle. "Only recently a few shop-assistants — a handful of counter-jumpers
— tried to shake the integrity of our commerse. But
their white cuffs held back their aarms, and the white
collars choked their aambitions." Contemplating parliamentary moves that will crush the unions, Ben dreams
of drapers secure in their citadels, enjoying a servile

labour force tamed by religious education. If union advances, dramatic in south Wales, troubled a Liberal Prime Minister, for Evans the coalfield communities held promise of a national regeneration. He said as much in 1916, when publicly supporting Welsh miners in their demands for higher wages. It wasn't a popular view, Lloyd George having proclaimed a wartime strike in the coal mines "unthinkable — quite unthinkable". As for Ben's nationalist affirmations ("Dear Wales... the land that is our heritage not by Act of Parliament but by Act of God", "Cymru Fydd — Wales for the Welsh — is here", "How sorry I am for any one who are not Welsh"), it needed no marked reorientation, as Evans saw it, for a Liberal leader set on furthering his political career to indulge the rhetoric of home rule, since nationalism was in the possession of those who, for all their talk of Welsh culture and the superior moral standards flowing from it, were at heart social reactionaries, craving British respectability. True to Evans's feelings about the type, Ben marries into English money and in his final deranged imaginings bends the knee before the English monarch. Interestingly, Ben the unprincipled opportunist, at once manipulator and puppet, accords with much in John Maynard Keynes's notorious portrait of the prime minister ("Lloyd George is rooted in nothing... he is an instrument and a player at the same time which plays on the company and is played on them too... a vampire and a medium in one"). Written also in 1919, Keynes's essay was not published until 1933, when it still gave offence.

"For Better", its title alluding to the marriage vows and marriage as mutually advantageous, has Ben, in return for Gwen's favours, scheming that her draper husband, the (impotent) Enos-Harries, be given the candidature of a Welsh constituency. The story clearly draws on Lloyd George's lengthy alliance with "Mrs Tim", the wife of Timothy Davies, a leading south-west London draper active in public life; backed by Lloyd George, he became in 1906 the Liberal MP for Fulham. The son born to Gwen hints at another affair of the late 1890s, this with a young married woman who brought a paternity suit against Lloyd George; successfully defended, it nonetheless provoked much gossip. Lloyd George, inevitably, remained in the eye of gossip and rumour, all of it open to Fleet Street where Evans had settled as sub-editor on the *Daily Mirror*.

Characteristically, Evans's blends horror with humour, the serious with the playful, and the black comedy pervasive in *My Neighbours*, a distinctive predatory mirth, marks his treatment of Ben. This man could talk his way out of Hell. Indeed, he does so in "The Two Apostles", an eschatological fantasy showing Judgement Day procedures derailed when the Welsh are called to account. In words, not deeds, do they trust, and this skittish piece confirms other constants in Evans's dissection of nation: the chapel's alliance with the secularly powerful, their joint oppression of the weak, a futile raging sectarianism, the unassailable spirit of the Elect, inexorably bound for Heaven: "'Ready am I, God bach,' Towy exclaimed, stretching his hairy arms. 'Take me.'" It was the author's enjoyment of his characters that struck the *TLS*; "though it is not desirable that every realist should be solemn," its review concluded, "every performer in literature… has to be serious, in the sense that he has to state events as he sees them; and this Mr Evans does".

The "realist" label was ever contentious when applied to Caradoc Evans, and particularly so in Wales, where critics argued that if realism meant a sense of proportion and believable natural speech, then Caradoc was never a realist. But fictional realism has other dimensions, not least a willingness to face uncomfortable social facts. *My Neighbours* touches on these in its many references to drapery, where Evans reveals an intimate, confident knowledge of shop practices and slang. Like Joseph ("Joseph's House"), he was put to drapery at fourteen, in the belief that here was a respectable haven for less robust country lads. In truth they entered a death trap, the death toll from tuberculosis amongst shop assistants exceeding rates for quarrymen and coalminers. "Living-in", with its disease-spreading dormitories, wretched wages, dismissal at a moment's notice, was a callous system of profit-making whereby assistants were paid partly in board and lodgings. Shop owners defended it in the name of morality and Christian guardianship — thus Enoch Harries' morning service ("I will not have atheists in my shop"). But David Rees fathers an illegitimate son ("Wisdom"), and an illegitimate son shot dead the owner of Whiteley's on the premises, the vast Bayswater store where Evans ended his decade in drapery. In theory, one could live out by getting married, but as this usually prompted dismissal, marriages were commonly kept secret (Jennie takes off her ring when returning to barracks). Men grew old living-in, the shop their only home, their personal relationships brutalised. P. C. Hoffman, like Caradoc's early mentor Duncan Davies, an activist in the struggle against living-in, tells of older assistants with money seeking out prostitutes; "Some caught disease in that way, and we would hear all about that, too." They might end up selling matches, laces and newspapers, their shabby respectable clothes and genteel mien proclaiming them no ordinary tramps. Rhys Hopkins ("The Lantern Bearer") mirrors just such a type.

195

An assumption of social superiority, the need to preserve a middle-class façade, made shop workers reluctant to speak out on working conditions no artisan would endure. A similar reticence characterized writers whose background was drapery, as H. G. Wells told a gathering of the Shop Assistants' Union. Caradoc Evans was his "brilliant exception", and *Nothing to Pay* (1930) the one true novel on what it meant to be a shop assistant. (Wells applauded its "brutal thoroughness" in exposing the injustices endured by shop workers, their savage rules of survival, their toadyism and lack of backbone.)

By autumn 1919 Evans had assembled the contents of *My Neighbours* for November publication: almost certainly fifteen stories, the number that had served for *My People*, and again for *Capel Sion*. At this point, so the evidence suggests, his publisher Andrew Melrose took fright at two of the pieces, "Wisdom" and "The Lantern Bearer". The latter's title possibly derives from "The Light of the World", Holman Hunt's immensely popular painting, a night scene lit by Christ's lantern, our guide in darkest places. A monstrous false religion, cloaking giant hypocrisies, infects the Kingsend store ruled by Enoch Harries. Robbed of a share in the business by this sinister buffoon, Rhys Hopkins becomes the lantern bearer, an overseer patrolling staff quarters on prurient nightly rounds; so begins a lust-driven downward spiral ending in vagrancy and religious delusion. Throughout, Rhys holds to the man who would destroy him — "Full of eloquence he is and plentiful blessings he has had" — and in a space above the premises seeks the essence of his master's sanctity: "he heard Harries praying, and he saw the words of the prayer coming through the floor in the shape of a spider's thread. The thread floated this way and that before it cleaved to the walls and roof of the garret." (A similar image appears in "Saint David and the Prophets".) As for Melrose's reaction, it was probably the diseased sexuality that most disturbed the sixty-year-old Scottish Presbyterian: Hopkins haunting the women's room, fingering discarded garments; gathering venereal blisters "at the mouths of dark alleys"; demented in Palewell Park, fondling a dying woman. "I strongly advise the deletion of this story," he wrote to the author. (Curiously, Evans jotted the phrase "creepy stories" on the back of his typescript, suggesting perhaps a foray into new fictional terrain.) Melrose's grounds for rejecting "Wisdom" are far less clear. A Welsh "merchant prince" in need of an heir; the consequent pressures on an aging man ("youth should begat; old age should frolic, inasmuch as it begets only weaklings"); a bastard son hidden in Wales; the male disregard of women (prized for dowries or as broodmares, else dangerous provokers of lust) — these are more familiar ingredients worked with verve and trenchancy. A wiser David Rees seeks reconciliation with his "boy chance", though only when assured of the young man's "wisdom", his canny way with money.

Whatever the reason, "Wisdom" touched a raw nerve in Melrose — "Is this story necessary?" he scrawled across the typescript — and Evans was not so committed to it or "The Lantern Bearer" as to ensure their retention. A seasoned editor himself, he knew that these were decisions for publishers who, like editors, backed their judgements in the marketplace, a forum he respected. Melrose's disquiet further extended to the Ben Lloyd stories, and shy of a possible libel action, he insisted that references to Ben's parliamentary career be excised through some last-minute cancels. In all, difficulties with the make-up of *My Neighbours* considerably delayed publication. Shorn of a couple of stories (restored in this present edition), bearing signs of hasty proofing, and with its "1919" title-page still intact, the book finally appeared in March 1920, mischievously close to St David's Day.

Reviews in England and Wales echoed those of the earlier collections. *The Bookman* neatly précised Evans's literary strengths: a fierce economy of prose, which packs a whole life-history into a single story; an absence of external comment, lending the narrative its stark, ironic appeal (the Old Testament debt was evident); and a playwright's approach to dialogue: "he depicts his characters solely by means of their conversation; and this conversation is always illuminating and dramatic". While praising its "devastating skill", *Punch* reported how the book had prompted threats of personal violence — "if I were the writer, I should purchase a bulldog," the reviewer signed off. Such sensationalist publicity, commonly generated by Evans, perturbed *The Nation*, since it allowed fiction of moral weight to be dismissed as "a sardonic kind of joke"; the writer's motives might be misunderstood, his assaults thought lacking in substance. Back home, the gloves were off from the start. The *Western Mail* cried "literary filth", "lewdness" and "obscenity", then more calmly voiced a common Welsh objection (even among those who, like the historian R. T. Jenkins, did not contest the factual basis of the stories), that the language talked in the book, that strange, compelling dialogue by which Evans sought to expose the socio-psychic life of his characters, rendered these characters ridiculous. Evans came back in due course, attack his preferred defence. "Your reviewer complains that the London Welsh characters in *My Neighbours* are stark idiots," begins his reply (22 March 1920):

*They are not. Idiocy is not the mark of Welsh Nonconformity. The mark is that of the knave, and the people of whom I have written are gutter knaves, who, when you turn your hose on them, howl out that of all people on earth there is none so clean.*

*Consider them. Consider the Welsh member of Parliament and his exploits: Summon him before you, and when you have examined him and uncovered his trickery, and wiped your feet on his garments, give him a pound note and he will depart blessing you. Dangle before him a golden carrot and he will trot merrily to hell.*

The letter recalls Llewelyn Williams, a prominent anti-Lloyd George Liberal, on the thirst for honours among Welsh MPs: "You get into the House to get on; you stay in to get honours; you get out to get honest."

Alone among Welsh newspapers, the *Carmarthen Journal* spoke up for Evans, its Anglican-Tory editor Lewis Giles doubtless once more relishing the Nonconformist discomfort an old friend's book had caused. "We consider that in Mr Caradoc Evans Wales has found her literary genius," ran the paper's front-page review, though it added the qualification, again one common in Wales, that however salutary his writings in his homeland, "the danger is that they may so influence the contempt of neighbouring nations as to set up a very serious handicap against Welsh national advancement". Evans knew the argument, that his books gave ammunition to the contemptuous English, and countered always by insisting that he cared enough for his country to tell the truth about her. It was a truth applicable in America where, as if to give weight to the *Carmarthen Journal's* further contention, that what this author was really exposing were the "phases of humbug and hypocrisy that are found in every nation", the critic H. L. Mencken seized on *My Neighbours'* relevance to a home-grown protestant fundamentalism.

"What we gather in our youth we commonly carry into our graves": the course of his early life shaped Evans's understanding of the world. Man's nature was hard, cruel and selfish, "though if you wait long enough you will see much that is good," he consoled his newspaper readers. Others would treat of that good; his task as writer was to make believable the side of life he knew, and this he did in stories that, once read, are not easily forgotten. In the words of Thomas Burke, a Fleet Street intimate and the dedicatee of *My Neighbours*, "They are, as all work should be, like nothing else. So was their author."

*John Harris*

# Note on the text

The texts of the thirteen stories of *My Neighbours* are largely as Andrew Melrose first published them. Obvious misprints have been silently corrected and there are slight changes in styling, mostly to bring hyphenation into line with modern practice. The New York edition of April 1920 (Harcourt, Brace & Howe) shows interesting differences. It adds a polemical preface, reorders the opening four stories, and offers some textual variants, in the Ben Lloyd stories particularly ("According to the Pattern" and "For Better"), where the intention is to make clear Ben's status as a member of parliament. In such instances, the American readings have been preferred.

The texts of "Wisdom" and "The Lantern Bearer" are taken from Evans's own typescripts, deposited in the National Library of Wales, Aberystwyth, as part of the Professor Gwyn Jones Papers. "Wisdom" was first printed in *Planet* 90 (1991/92); "The Lantern Bearer" has not been previously published.

Four stories in *My Neighbours* originally appeared as follows:

"A Widow Woman", *Westminster Gazette*, 2 June 1917, pp. 1-2 (as "A Widow Woman in Sion").

"Treasure and Trouble", *Westminster Gazette*, 15 September 1917, pp. 1-2.

"Earthbred", *English Review*, March 1918, pp. 227-33 (as "Earthbred: A Study of the London Welsh").

"Joseph's House", *English Review*, August 1919, pp. 141-47.